D0933121

"Welcome to the other side of Sunset Island," Kurt said tersely.

Carrie was horrified. "Who lives here?"

"Lots of people," Kurt said, getting out of the Jeep. "Just not people the tourists want to acknowledge."

"I can't believe I've spent so much time on the island without knowing this part of it existed," Carrie began.

She assembled her equipment and climbed out after him. It's my responsibility to take pictures of this, she thought. It may not be pretty, and some people might not want to look at it, but real photojournalists tell the whole story, and I'm going to be a real photojournalist.

The SUNSET ISLAND series
by Cherie Bennett

Sunset Island
Sunset Kiss
Sunset Dreams
Sunset Farewell
Sunset Reunion
Sunset Secrets
Sunset Heat
Sunset Promises

Sunset Promises

Cherie Bennett

SPLASH™

A BERKLEY / SPLASH BOOK

SUNSET PROMISES is an original publication of
The Berkley Publishing Group.
This work has never appeared before in book form.

SUNSET PROMISES

A Berkley Book / published by arrangement with
General Licensing Company, Inc.

PRINTING HISTORY
Berkley edition / July 1992

All rights reserved.
Copyright © 1992 by General Licensing Company, Inc.
Cover art copyright © 1992 by General Licensing Company, Inc.
This book may not be reproduced in whole or in part,
by mimeograph or any other means, without permission.
For information address: General Licensing Company, Inc.,
24 West 25th Street, New York, New York 10010.

A GLC BOOK

Splash is a registered trademark of
General Licensing Company, Inc.

ISBN: 0-425-13384-2

A BERKLEY BOOK ® TM 757,375
Berkley Books are published by The Berkley Publishing Group,
200 Madison Avenue, New York, New York 10016.
The name "BERKLEY" and the "B" logo
are trademarks belonging to Berkley Publishing Corporation.

PRINTED IN THE UNITED STATES OF AMERICA

10 9 8 7 6 5 4 3 2 1

For Jeff

ONE

"How about if I spread suntan lotion on your back?" Billy asked Carrie as she turned over on the blanket they had spread out on the beach. "And after that, I could do the front," he offered.

Carrie laughed as she felt Billy's warm hand firmly rub the cream into her back. "You're such an obliging guy," she teased.

"I try," Billy murmured, stroking the last of the lotion into Carrie's skin.

Carrie closed her eyes and let the feeling of Billy's hand and the warm sun beating down on her back lull her for a moment.

Bliss. Sheer bliss, Carrie thought. *Billy Sampson—the lead singer of Flirting with Danger, not to mention the cutest, coolest guy I know—is rubbing my back. I'm working on Sunset Island, one of the most gor-*

geous places in the world, in a job I love. I'm hanging out with my two best friends, Samantha Bridges and Emma Cresswell, for the entire summer. I don't even have to think about going back to Yale, studying, or tuition problems for months. Bliss.

"This bathing suit looks great on you," Billy said softly as his hand caressed the skin under the neck strap of her blue bathing suit. "Did I mention that?"

"Just two or three times," Carrie said with a happy smile. Since she often felt insecure about her naturally curvaceous figure (which would never be a size six, like Emma's), this compliment filled her with happiness. Evidently Billy Sampson thought she looked just fine.

"Hey, Carrie," Billy called, and Carrie lifted her head off the blanket. Billy snapped off two or three photos with his Cannon camera.

"My face is probably all creased from the blanket!" Carrie protested.

"Nope," Billy assured her, clicking off a few more shots. "Not at all. And having the sun behind you like that creates a great effect."

Carrie smiled shyly at the camera as Billy stood up to get a different angle.

It was photography that had brought Billy and Carrie together in the first place. They had met on the island the previous summer when Carrie noticed the great camera that Billy had around his neck. Carrie had been about to start her freshman year at Yale, and hoped to become a photojournalist. And while Billy was best known as a hot singer, he also had a passion for photography and was learning more about it every day.

Carrie had been so attracted to Billy that at first she'd found it difficult even to make conversation with him. She had also found it impossible to believe that the hottest guy on the island, the lead singer of the Flirts, actually would be interested in her.

"You're cute and nice and mega-smart," Sam had told Carrie the summer before when she'd expressed her doubts about Billy's feelings for her. "What's not to like?"

But I'm not cute compared to you or Emma—that was what Carrie had felt like saying to Sam last summer.

Although Carrie wouldn't admit it out loud, sometimes it was tough being best friends with Sam and Emma. They were both so outstanding. Emma Cresswell was a beautiful, perfect-looking Boston heiress

3

who had traveled all over the world and spoke five languages, and Sam Bridges was a tall, gorgeous, wild-looking model type who drove guys insane.

And then there's me, Carrie thought with a sigh. Nice, girl-next-door, hard-working, level-headed Carrie. In fact, when Carrie had first met Billy, she'd been so convinced that he couldn't possibly want her as she was that she'd made herself over into what she *thought* he wanted her to be. Carrie had piled on the eye makeup and lipstick, bought some wild, low-cut outfits and high heels, and even gotten drunk at a recording-studio party he'd taken her to. It had turned out that Billy really liked Carrie for who she was, not who she was pretending to be, and her games had almost ruined their fledgling relationship. Now that they were still an item a whole year later, Carrie was really glad that she'd found out the truth in time.

"What are you smiling about?" Billy asked as he clicked off another shot of her.

"Life," Carrie answered enigmatically. She sat up and pushed her hair out of her face. "Hey, do I get to take some of you, too?" she asked, putting out her hand for the camera.

"I know you," Billy said, feinting back and

still shooting. "You'll focus on the ocean or the seagulls or something, instead of me. Hey, shade one side of your face with your hand. I want to see what effect the shadow will produce," he added.

Carrie obliged, thinking that Billy was right. She did love to take photographs of Sunset Island landscape, and she often preferred those to portrait shots. "You get your picture taken by screaming groupies all the time," Carrie teased him. "You don't need any more pictures of yourself."

"I'm ready for my closeup!" a voice called from the sand. Carrie turned around. It was Sam, loping toward them in a polka-dot bikini that fit her to perfection.

"Hey, get a shot of this!" Sam suggested as she dropped down next to Carrie and put her face next to her friend's. Billy snapped away.

"You look great," Carrie said, eyeing Sam's skinny midriff. She looked down at her own royal blue maillot and hoped she didn't look like a whale in comparison.

"I got this at the Cheap Boutique yesterday," Sam said, naming the best place on the island to get hip, relatively inexpensive clothes. "Mr. Jacobs gave me a bonus for taking the monsters to the twins picnic in

Bangor. Believe me, I earned every penny of it."

The monsters Sam was referring to were Becky and Allie Jacobs, the fourteen-year-old identical twins that were in her charge. They were wildly precocious and quite a handful.

"I'm glad I ran into you," Sam said, digging her toes into the sand. "You may find this hard to believe, but the twins are giving a party tomorrow night, and they want to invite Ian."

"Ian?" Carrie echoed in surprise. Ian Templeton was the thirteen-year-old son of Graham and Claudia Templeton and one of the two kids that Carrie was taking care of for the summer. Ian's dad, known in the rock world as Graham Perry, was a rock-and-roll legend. Carrie still found it hard to believe that she worked for him. She'd even had the opportunity to have some of her photos of him and his band published in *Rock On* magazine.

"I know what you're thinking," Sam said. "Becky and Allie usually won't even look at a guy unless he's old enough to have a driver's license, but Ian is the son of you-know-who, so I guess they're making an exception."

Billy lowered the camera and dropped

down next to Carrie. "That's a drag, inviting the kid just because his old man is famous."

"I agree," Carrie said. "And Ian is such a sweet, sensitive kid. Maybe you could talk the twins out of it."

Sam laughed and let some sand sift between her fingers. "Have you ever tried to talk the twins into or out of anything? I'd have better luck mediating the Middle East peace talks."

"Hey, Sam, we're ready to go!" one of the twins yelled impatiently from the boardwalk.

"Duty calls," Sam said, standing up and brushing the sand off her legs. "So you'll see if you can get Ian to go to this party?"

"I suppose so," Carrie agreed reluctantly.

"Thanks," Sam said. She turned around, and then turned back. "Oh, hey, I got a letter from Marina today."

Sam was referring to Marina Mazzetti, a dancer from New York who had come to Sunset Island earlier that summer to work as a lifeguard at the country club. Marina and Sam had both been hired by a company called Show World International to dance in a revue in Japan. Marina had gone overseas a month before Sam, and had called her in desperation to tell her that the whole thing

7

was a big scam, little more than a front for prostitution. Marina had been stranded and scared, and Sam had arranged to borrow the money from Emma to get Marina back to the United States.

"How's she doing?" Carrie asked. She had really liked Marina. They all had.

"She's back in New York at her old job, teaching aerobics at the Vertical Club," Sam said. "She's coaching some rich ladies privately so she can start paying Emma back."

"Sam! I've got phone calls to make!" one of the twins bellowed irritably from the boardwalk.

"Yo, patience is a virtue!" Sam yelled back. "Honestly, Allie was easier to live with during her spiritual phase," she sighed. "Anyhow, I'm going to write back to Marina tonight."

"You'll never mail the letter," Carrie said with a laugh. Sam was famous for writing letters she never mailed. She'd told Carrie she'd written six or seven to her at Yale that Carrie had never seen.

"So I'll call when the rates are low," Sam said with a shrug. "Catch you later!"

Billy shook his hair out of his face and watched Sam walk away. "She's one of a kind. Nothing ever bothers her."

"Mmm," Carrie answered noncommittally. She knew that wasn't true at all. Sam only acted like nothing ever bothered her. In fact, Carrie knew that Sam was going through a very difficult time at the moment. When she'd been hired for the job dancing overseas, she'd had her younger sister, Ruth Ann, send her her birth certificate so she could get a passport. But when the certificate arrived, it revealed that Sam had been adopted, something her parents had never told her. Now Sam was struggling with her feelings of hurt and anger.

"Maybe we should all get together and send Marina a card or something," Billy suggested. Carrie knew he'd liked Marina, too.

"Speaking of cards," Carrie said lightly, "I got one from Josh yesterday." Josh was Carrie's longtime high school boyfriend. They were both students at Yale, and Carrie was torn between her love for Josh and her lust for Billy. Josh seemed more like a brother to Carrie now, but he wanted to be much more than that. She'd always been very up-front with Billy about Josh, and vice versa.

"Cool," Billy said, lying down on his back and folding his arms over his chest. He closed his eyes against the sun.

Carrie propped herself on one elbow next to him. "I only mention it because . . . well, he wants to come visit."

"Is that right?" Billy asked without opening his eyes.

"In a few days, actually," Carrie continued. "He's got some time off from his summer job. So . . . I was wondering how you would feel about that."

Billy opened his eyes and shaded them with his hand. He gave Carrie a thoughtful look. "That's a question you should be asking yourself, not me."

"But you must have an opinion," Carrie pressed.

Billy closed his eyes again. "Maybe," he allowed. "But I'm not giving it."

"Why not?" Carrie asked in frustration. "If I didn't care about how you feel, I wouldn't ask you."

Billy turned to look at Carrie. "It's got to be your decision," he said implacably.

Carrie wasn't sure what to say. Billy was so totally unlike Josh, and Josh was the only boyfriend she'd ever had before Billy. Josh got jealous if Carrie so much as talked to another guy. Now here was Billy, not reacting at all to the possibility that her old flame might show up on Sunset Island! Carrie knew for sure that if one of Billy's old girlfriends showed up on the island, she'd want to kill her. Did that mean Billy didn't really care about her as much as she cared about him?

"So you won't say anything about it at all?" Carrie asked.

"Like I said," Billy repeated, "it's up to you. I'll feel the same way about you, either way."

Later, Carrie replayed that line over and over in her mind as she headed back to the Templetons'. What had Billy meant when he said that he'd feel the same either way? How was it possible for him to really care about her and not get jealous if Josh showed up?

"Hey, you really got some color," Ian said when Carrie walked in the front door. He was struggling to carry an empty washing-machine cylinder into the playroom.

"I'll help you," Carrie said, grabbing the other side.

"I can do it!" Ian protested. He was small and thin for his age, and very sensitive about it.

"I'm sure you can, but this will just help you balance it," Carrie said smoothly as they maneuvered the hulking washing-machine part into the room.

11

"My newest instrument," Ian said proudly.

"Great!" Carrie said, trying to sound enthusiastic. Recently Ian had formed his own band, called Lord Whitehead and the Zit Men. They played what Ian called industrial music. The band used brushes and sticks to make music on various household appliances—a microwave, a dishwasher, and now a washing machine. Ian was very proud of the originality of this concept. Carrie secretly was afraid that this was just Ian's way of creating music without competing with his superstar father.

"The band is having a practice here tomorrow," Ian said with excitement. "Want to watch?"

"Sure," Carrie agreed. She couldn't imagine what kind of music could come from a washing machine, but she hoped for Ian's sake that it would be better than she thought it would.

"Hey, can we have pizza for dinner?" Ian asked. "Mom and Dad went to the studio in Bangor."

"Who's with Chloe, then?" Carrie asked in surprise. Graham and Claudia had known she wouldn't be back until this time, and Chloe was only five years old.

"Ian's with me!" Chloe chirped from the doorway.

"They just left about five minutes ago, so they knew you'd be right back," Ian said.

Good thing I didn't get a flat tire or something, Carrie thought. Sometimes she thought she was more responsible than the people she worked for.

"I want pizza for dinner, too," Chloe said. "And ice cream."

"Oh, you do, do you?" Carrie teased, advancing on Chloe. She tickled the little girl until Chloe squealed with delight.

"No more tickle monster!" Chloe yelped.

"Okay," Carrie agreed, swooping the little girl up for a big kiss. Chloe was the sweetest of kids, and Carrie really loved her. "Ice-cream-flavored pizza for dinner," she agreed. "And pizza-flavored ice cream for dessert."

"You're so silly." Chloe giggled. "I'll get the pizza place's number!" Chloe ran into the kitchen to get the pizza menu from the bulletin board.

As Carrie looked over the menu her mind wasn't really on mushrooms and pepperoni. Her thoughts were of Billy and what he'd said to her at the beach. *It's up to you*, he'd said without blinking an eye. Carrie felt a bubble of anxiety well up in her stomach. *No way could a guy say that if he was crazy about a girl*, she thought with dread. *It just isn't possible.*

Suddenly Carrie had completely lost her appetite.

TWO

"Carrie, should I wear my red shoes or my blue shoes?" Chloe asked with a real note of concern in her voice.

Good grief, Carrie thought. *This five-year-old pays as much attention to how she dresses for a date as I do. Maybe more.*

Carrie watched Chloe put a red shoe on her left foot and a blue one on her right before responding. "Really, Chloe," she said. "You're going to a play date at your friend Annie's house, not to a party. Maybe you should wear your sneakers."

Chloe made a face. "Ugh. Not sneakers. I want to look pretty for Annie's grandma. Okay, I'll wear the red ones."

As Carrie helped Chloe tie her shoelaces she thought back to the previous day, when she had taken Chloe for her swimming lesson and Chloe had found herself in the same swimming class with Annie McWilliams. The two children had immediately become fast friends when Kurt Ackerman, Emma's boyfriend and the country club swim instructor who was teaching the class, had them stick their heads underwater and then pop up inside an inflatable duck-shaped swim ring. For some reason, Chloe and Annie both had found this hilarious.

When they had finally come out of the pool, Chloe had insisted stubbornly that Annie come over and meet Carrie. That was when an impeccably dressed, perfectly coiffed older woman had walked over to Carrie and the two small girls.

"Is that darling child yours?" she had asked Carrie as she took Annie by the hand.

"Well, sort of," Carrie had replied. "I'm Carrie Alden, and I'm Chloe's au pair."

"I'm May Spencer-Rumsey," the tall, gray-haired woman had said, drying Annie off. "I'm Annie McWilliams's grandmother. And it seems to me that my granddaughter and your charge are well on their way to becoming inseparable."

Carrie had chuckled as she slipped Chloe's coverup over the child's head. *I like this woman*, she thought. *She's so well-spoken.*

"So what I'd like to propose, Miss Alden,

is that you bring Chloe over to my home tomorrow, and the two of them can have what my daughter—Annie's mother—calls a quality-time play date." She had smiled. "I prefer to think of it as two children spending the afternoon together."

Carrie, seeing Chloe and Annie already settling down together to color in the coloring books they had brought to the club, had thought it might be a good idea. She had told Ms. Spencer-Rumsey that she would clear it with her employers and call her that evening. Ms. Spencer-Rumsey had given her the phone number and written down her address.

Except it wasn't an address. All she had written was *Winterhaven.*

"Winterhaven?" Carrie had asked.

"Oh, that's my home," Ms. Spencer-Rumsey had said easily. "Just ask anyone where it is."

That night, Claudia Templeton had given her permission to take Chloe to Winterhaven. "Winterhaven!" she'd exclaimed with a laugh. "I didn't think they even let children onto that estate." She had given Carrie directions and said that if she got lost, she should just look for the white house with the long driveway on the far end of Shore Road.

Which was why Carrie was helping Chloe select her shoes. Once Chloe was finally dressed, Carrie loaded her and a big bag of toys into the Templetons' Mercedes and made the short drive to Winterhaven. Winterhaven, it turned out, didn't have an ordinary long driveway. It basically had a private road leading to it.

When Carrie pulled up in front of a huge white mansion, Ms. Spencer-Rumsey and Annie were waiting on the front porch. A uniformed young man took the Mercedes to park it.

"Welcome to Winterhaven," Ms. Spencer-Rumsey said with a warm smile.

Chloe smiled shyly at her new friend. "I brought toys," she said.

"But I've got toys," Annie answered.

Chloe looked disappointed.

"But I like your toys better," Annie amended quickly.

Carrie and Ms. Spencer-Rumsey shared a smile.

"Annie's been waiting for Chloe to arrive," Ms. Spencer-Rumsey said. "Why don't we let the two of them play upstairs in Annie's room? I'll give you a tour of the place."

"Have fun," Carrie told Chloe as the little girl went skipping off with Annie.

Jeez, this place is fantastic, Carrie thought as Annie's grandmother showed her around. *It's got to have thirty rooms!* She marveled at how Winterhaven was situated on a small peninsula jutting into the Atlantic Ocean, the sea crashing spectacularly over a picturesque seawall below the house. "You know, Ms. Spencer-Rumsey, I'd love to come out here and take photographs sometime—that is, if you wouldn't mind," Carrie said as they sat by a picture window, taking in the scene.

"Please call me May," Ms. Spencer-Rumsey replied. "And I wouldn't mind at all. So, you enjoy photography?"

"I love it!" Carrie said.

"Then come with me," May said. "I want to show you something." She arose, walked down a long hallway, and turned into a room. Carrie followed.

When May flipped on the lights, Carrie's jaw dropped. The walls were covered with framed photographs. But not just any photographs. There were prints by the likes of Alfred Stieglitz, Walker Evans, Ansel Adams, and even Diane Arbus.

May saw Carrie's reaction and laughed. "I see you know pictures," she said.

"A little," Carrie replied. "These are

amazing." *Good lord*, Carrie thought, *there's a David Frohman hanging over there. That must have cost a zillion dollars.*

"The Frohman was purchased at a Christie's auction last year," May continued, seeing Carrie gazing at the photograph.

"I love his work," Carrie murmured, speaking half to herself. "One day, I'd like to be as good as he is."

May nodded with approval. "Well, that's just the attitude you need to succeed in life," she said.

As much as looking at the photos mesmerized Carrie, she felt uneasy that Chloe had been out of her sight for so long.

"Do you think we should go check on the kids?" Carrie asked. "When Chloe's this quiet, it makes me nervous."

"I know the feeling!" May said with a laugh. "Come on." She led the way up a spiral staircase to Annie's room, where they found the two girls putting on makeup and admiring themselves in a small mirror.

"Go away, we're having fun," Chloe said when she saw Carrie.

"Yeah, fun," Annie piped up.

"Carrie," May said in a hurt tone of voice but with a twinkle in her eye, "I can see these two big girls here don't want us around. Let's go down to the kitchen and I'll make us some lemonade. Annie, do you want some?"

Annie didn't look away from the mirror as she applied lipstick to her chin. "No, Grandma. Later, okay?"

"How about you, Chloe? Are you hungry or thirsty?"

"No, thank you," Chloe responded politely, putting blush on her forehead.

"Carrie?" May said with a smile.

"Okay!" Carrie replied smartly, and the two of them laughed as they went downstairs.

Drinking lemonade, Carrie found it easy to talk to Ms. Spencer-Rumsey, at least when the subject was photography. Carrie told her about some of the photos she had taken of Sunset Island, of the success that she'd had already with *Rock On* magazine, and even about her ambition to become a photojournalist.

May smiled when Carrie told her about her career plans. "When you're ready, Carrie, I'd be delighted to take a look at some of your prints. I don't know if I mentioned this before, but back in New York, my family runs the Spencer Publishing Group."

Carrie almost choked on her lemonade.

The Spencer Publishing Group! Why didn't I make the connection before? she thought. *That's the most famous photography publishing house in the world.*

"That would be nothing short of fantastic," Carrie said honestly. "Your publishing house is very well known. I'm sure you know what's really good."

"It's funny that you mentioned wanting to take photos around Winterhaven," May said. "I've been thinking for some time of publishing a coffee-table volume called *The World of Sunset Island*. I think it would be magnificent, don't you?"

"Absolutely," Carrie agreed. "It's so beautiful here. I think the whole world should see this island."

May grinned, finished the last of her lemonade, and stood up. "So, Carrie," she said, heading back to the staircase, "why don't you bring some of your Sunset Island prints the next time you bring Chloe over to play with Annie? I'll give them a careful look; perhaps they'll be appropriate for the book."

Carrie was dumbstruck for a moment, but stood up and followed May. *Omigod, omigod, my photos in a Spencer book!* She shook her head. *Now wait. All she wants to do is look at them. And I'm still mostly an amateur.*

"Thank you, May. I'd like that very much," Carrie replied.

And while she cleaned up Chloe, gathered her toys, thanked May Spencer-Rumsey for the wonderful afternoon, and then drove the two of them back home, all she could think of was having her pictures in *The World of Sunset Island.*

By the time they arrived back at the Templetons', it was already late in the afternoon. Parked in the Templetons' driveway was an assortment of minibikes and bicycles, and one large supermarket shopping cart. *Must be some of Ian's friends,* Carrie thought. *But I don't get the shopping cart at all!*

After she unloaded Chloe, she walked into the kitchen, where Claudia Templeton was cutting up onions and green peppers for a dinner quiche.

"How'd it go?" Claudia asked as she sliced.

"Pretty well," Carrie said cheerfully. "Just be careful that your daughter doesn't grow up to be an Avon lady!" Carrie told Claudia about Chloe and Annie's adventures with cosmetics.

"Well," Claudia said, "maybe an Avon lady

23

isn't so bad. It'd be better than another rock star in the family! Speaking of which, Ian's down in the basement rehearsing with his band. Would you please go check on them?"

"Sure." Carrie smiled and got up from the table. "Uh, Claudia, do you know there's a shopping cart in the driveway?"

Claudia smiled back. "It's for their instruments, Carrie."

Carrie looked puzzled.

"Seeing is believing," Claudia said. She shook her head as she went back to cutting vegetables. Carrie got the feeling that Claudia didn't think very much of Ian's musical endeavors.

When Carrie went down to the basement, she found four teenage boys (all Ian's age and all dressed in white painter's caps, black jeans, black boots, and flesh-colored long-sleeved T-shirts), one huge tape deck-amp-speaker combination, and a collection of broken appliances obviously salvaged from the Sunset Island town dump.

Ian was huddled in deep discussion with the other boys when Carrie came in. His face lit up when he saw her.

"Guys," he said to them importantly, "this is Carrie Alden. She takes care of Chloe. Carrie, this is my band, the all-new Lord

Whitehead and the Zit Men. These are the Zits." Ian motioned to the three guys sitting on the basement floor near him. Carrie could tell from the expression of their faces that they were very impressed with the fact that they were sitting on Graham Perry's basement floor.

What do you say when you're introduced to three thirteen-year-old Zits? Carrie thought. Then, to stop herself from laughing, she said, "Tell me your names and what instruments you guys play."

Ian folded his arms self-importantly. Obviously, he was the leader, and no one spoke until he did. He motioned to the group. "From left to right, there's William 'Refrigerator' Kerry on fridge, Donald Zuckerman on microwave and toaster oven, and Marcus Woods on Mr. Coffee and Cuisinart." Each boy nodded in turn when Ian introduced him. "I play the washing machine," he added, pointing to the hollowed-out hulk that Carrie had helped carry downstairs the day before.

"I see," said Carrie, trying to keep a straight face. "Well, I'll just sit here and, uh . . . listen. Okay?"

"Sure thing," Ian said, walking over to the tape deck and starting to fumble through a wicker basket filled with cassette tapes. "Guys, assume your positions!"

The Zit Men scrambled to their respective places and awaited further instructions from Ian. *Oh, no!* Carrie realized as she watched them from the basement steps. *Those outfits are supposed to make them look like pimples!*

"Let's try Bowie's 'Suffragette City,'" Ian said.

"Don't know it," Donald said, crestfallen.

"Okay, let's do 'Holiday in Cambodia' by the DK's," Ian suggested.

"Uh, don't know it," William said in a quiet voice.

"Doesn't matter," Ian said as he shuffled through the tapes in the basket. "Okay! I've got it! A classic! 'Louie Louie!'"

Marcus looked very unhappy. "Ian," he said, "I don't know that one."

Carrie saw an exasperated look cross Ian's face. The session obviously was not going the way he had intended.

"Look, guys," Ian said with a supercilious look at his bandmates, "we're all serious musicians here. I'm going to put in a tape, and let's just jam!"

Ian popped a tape in the cassette player. Carrie recognized Elton John's "Crocodile

Rock" blaring out over the speakers—but just for a moment, because almost instantly, the sounds of Elton John were obliterated in a cacophony of metallic banging and rattling that made Carrie feel like she was visiting a Pittsburgh steel mill.

Mercifully, the song ended prematurely when Ian stopped the tape. Carrie watched him walk over to Marcus and give him some instruction on how he should beat the inside of his Cuisinart. Then Ian walked right up to Carrie.

"What do you think?" he asked proudly.

Carrie could hear her friend Sam's voice in her head. *Tell him that you think he must have inherited his mother's genes instead of his father's! Tell him he shouldn't quit his day job!*

But Carrie was much more diplomatic than Sam. "I think your music has a lot of originality and a lot of potential," she said with a straight face. "But I also think you could use a bit more practice."

Ian fairly whooped around the room. "Didja hear that, guys?" he chortled. "She likes it! She likes it! Now, let's get back to work. Excuse me, Carrie, but the last part of this rehearsal is closed to the public."

Carrie grinned inwardly, winked to Ian

that she understood, and went back upstairs. When she got to her room, she was
laughing so hard, tears filled her eyes.

After Claudia had served a delicious veg-
etarian quiche for dinner, Carrie went back
up to her room. Thoughts of Josh were
filling her head. Should she invite him to
come? Did Billy care one way or the other?
She took Josh's card out of her purse and
read it over again.

*I can visit as a friend, or as something
more,* Josh had written, *but this going all
summer without seeing each other is stupid.
I really miss you.*

Did she miss Josh? The truth was that she
did. But she missed him the way she might
miss Sam or Emma, not the way she missed
Billy when she wasn't with him. But Billy
was being so blasé—maybe the best thing
she could do would be to shake him up by
inviting Josh. On the other hand, she
thought, that wouldn't be fair to Josh. There
just didn't seem to be any chemistry between them anymore. But she remembered
how it used to be between them in high
school. They could hardly keep their hands
off each other. So what did it all mean,
anyway?

"Stop thinking!" Carrie ordered herself out loud. "Just do something!"

Carrie marched to the phone and dialed Josh's number.

"Carrie!" he cried when he answered. "I'm so glad you called. It's great to hear your voice. I've missed you."

And at that moment, Carrie missed him, too. *If I were with him in New Jersey and I told him that Billy was going to come visit me, Josh wouldn't take it lying down.*

"Josh, I was thinking about your letter," Carrie said, playing nervously with the phone cord.

"Um, what is it you were thinking about it?" Josh answered, a note of fear in his voice. *He thinks I'm going to reject him!* Carrie realized.

"Well, about your coming up here to visit for a few days—" Carrie began.

"You don't think it's a good idea?" Josh interrupted, sounding more fearful than ever.

"I think it's a terrific idea!" Carrie said with all the enthusiasm she could muster.

"That's great!" Josh cried, and Carrie could hear the relief in his voice. "Like I said in the letter, I can get a plane tomorrow and be on the six o'clock ferry."

"I'll meet you," Carrie promised.

"I can't wait to see you," Josh said in a low voice.

"Josh, I'm . . . I'm not sure what this visit is going to be, okay?" Carrie said, trying to get the awkward words to make sense. "I mean, my situation hasn't really changed."

"Meaning Billy," Josh said in a steely voice.

"Right," Carrie agreed.

"Look, as far as I'm concerned, you're not married, you're not engaged, and you can do what you want," Josh said. "That includes seeing the guy who's been in love with you and stood by you for five whole years."

"I do want to see you," Carrie told him. "It's just . . . well, I can't lie to you about it."

"That's my girl, honest to a fault," Josh said, trying for some levity. "As long as I don't have to see you two together—you wouldn't pull that, would you?"

"No," Carrie said, "I wouldn't."

"Then we're cool," Josh concluded.

Carrie only half listened to the rest of what Josh had to say, and she hung up with anxiety eating at her stomach. One part of her wanted to show Josh the island, to be with him and have fun, but another part of her thought she was absolutely nuts to jeopardize one second of her time with Billy, or to do anything as immature as trying to make Billy jealous.

What am I getting myself into? she wondered after she hung up. *Josh on one side of me, Billy on the other. Looks like it's going to be a Carrie Alden sandwich, and I'm the one who's definitely going to be the dead meat in the middle.*

THREE

"This shot of Billy's buns is to die for," Sam said, picking up a photo that Carrie had taken of Billy on the beach, running toward the ocean.

"Oops, wrong pile," Carrie said, retrieving the photo of Billy and putting it back in her portfolio.

"But that was Sam's favorite!" Emma teased.

"You're supposed to be helping me pick photos of the island to show Ms. Spencer-Rumsey, and I don't think Billy qualifies," Carrie reminded them.

The three girls were sitting on Carrie's bed later that day, going through Carrie's photos. She had told them all about her conversation with the famous publisher, and they'd come over to help her choose which photos to show May.

"You think she meant it about looking at my photos, or do you think she was just being nice?" Carrie asked as she pulled the next shot out of her leather case.

"When you're that rich, you don't have to be nice," Sam opined. Seeing Emma's cool look, Sam went on, "Present company excluded, of course, Emma. You're genuinely nice even though you have enough money to tell the entire world to kiss off." She pulled another photo out of Carrie's portfolio. "Sunset on the dunes. Now, this one is fabulous."

"I agree," Emma said. "The shadows are beautiful."

"You think?" Carrie said, scrutinizing the shot.

Sam stared at Carrie. "Carrie Alden doubting herself? Can it be?"

"Oh, everyone has doubts sometimes," Carrie said.

"Not me," Sam said.

"That's total bull." Emma laughed. "You doubt yourself just as much as we do. You simply hide it better."

Sam reached for some chips from the bowl on the bed. Her face grew thoughtful, then sad.

"Oh, hey, Emma didn't mean anything . . ." Carrie began, but didn't finish the sentence.

"You know I didn't," Emma said to Sam quietly.

"I know," Sam agreed.

"How's it going with your parents, anyway?" Carrie asked.

Sam shrugged. "We're speaking, that's about all I can say."

"Well, it's a start," Emma said kindly.

"I guess," Sam said. "But I still get these incredibly angry feelings because they didn't tell me the truth all these years. Sometimes I just feel like exploding."

Emma and Carrie nodded in sympathy.

Sam looked at her friends' serious faces and burst out laughing. "If you could just see the two of you! Look, I'm dealing with it, okay? Let's look at the photos and decide which ones are going to make Carrie a star."

They sifted through some more shots until Sam realized how late it was and jumped off the bed. "Oh, wow, I've got to get back for the monsters' party. I promised Mr. Jacobs I'd help the twins choose their outfits," she said, rolling her eyes. "Sure. Like the twins are going to let anyone choose anything for them." She grabbed the last two chips from the bowl and popped them in her mouth, grabbing her purse on her way out the door. "So you'll be over later?" Sam asked Carrie.

Carrie nodded. "I'll drive Ian over about eight," she said. "He's incredibly excited and trying to act very blasé."

"You sure you can't come, Emma?" Sam asked, hoisting her shoulder bag up on her arm.

"Sorry," Emma said. "I have to stay with the kids tonight."

Sam laughed. "Sorry, my butt! You know you'd rather stay with the darling Hewitt kids then help supervise this little shindig," she said. "Can't say that I blame you, either. Catch you later!"

Carrie and Emma spent another half-hour with Carrie's photos, then Emma left and Carrie got ready to take Ian to the party. When she finished showering and changing, Ian was waiting for her downstairs in the kitchen. He had on his Lord Whitehead band outfit.

"Hey, this looks okay, right?" Ian asked nervously.

"Well, it's . . . um . . . it makes a

statement," Carrie said, taking in the flesh-colored shirt and the white hat.

"Making a statement is good, right?" Ian asked.

"Sometimes," Carrie commented. "Maybe you should just leave off the hat, since no one will know this is your band's outfit."

Ian frowned and took off his hat. He stared at it. "Well, I figured if I wore the hat, people might ask why I was wearing it, and then I could tell everyone about my band."

"Good point," Carrie said seriously. She knew the kid should lose the hat, but she wasn't sure how to tell him. She didn't want to make him any more nervous or self-conscious than he already was.

"A lot of older kids will be there," Ian said, twirling his hat on his finger. "Like sixteen-year-olds, and some even older."

Carrie nodded. Ian stared at the hat on his finger and finally set it down on the kitchen table. "I wish I weren't so short," he mumbled. "It sucks."

Carrie made small talk with Ian as they drove over to the Jacobses' house. She felt sorry for him. He was such a sweet kid, and it was so hard for him to be the son of a superstar.

"Hey, do you think Allie and Becky invited me because of who my dad is?" Ian asked suddenly.

"I don't know," Carrie said honestly. She saw Ian's face fall and she winced inside. Why did she have to be so honest? "I mean, I'm sure they like you," Carrie added. "You're extremely likeable."

"I'm also extremely short," Ian said with a sigh.

"You know, your dad isn't short," Carrie pointed out as she stopped at a light. "So I think it's pretty likely you're going to get tall in a few years."

"Maybe," Ian said doubtfully. "Meanwhile I'll be permanently scarred from being a shrimp during my formative years."

Carrie laughed and pulled the car into the Jacobses' driveway. She glanced at Ian. He looked really nervous. Loud rap music was blasting from the house, and two guys who looked like high school football players were just crowding in the front door. Ian shot Carrie a panicky look.

"How about if I go park so you can go in by yourself?" Carrie suggested. She realized that it would be embarrassing for him to walk in with her.

"Oh, yeah, good idea," Ian said gratefully. "So, I'll see you inside." He got out of the car and headed for the front door.

When Carrie walked into the Jacobses' house, she was hit by a wall of sound. There seemed to be a zillion teenage bodies in the house, all yelling and screeching over the rap music. She caught sight of Sam's red curls over the heads of some gyrating dancers and waved in her direction.

"Welcome to the zoo," Sam yelled when Carrie had made her way across the family room. "I think every kid on the island between the ages of fourteen and seventeen is here."

"I didn't know the twins were so popular," Carrie said.

"Well, they told everyone that their dad would be away, so it would be a really good party," Sam said, rolling her eyes.

"I'm surprised he let them give a party when he's away," Carrie said.

"Oh, he's only 'away' for a few hours. He's not out of town. It's their version of a white lie."

"Sam, we are, like, completely out of food already," Becky yelled, coming up to Sam. "Can we order some pizzas?"

"They already ate all those sandwiches I made?" Sam asked.

"Well, somebody danced into the table and about fifty of them fell on the floor," Becky yelled. "I told you sandwiches were a stupid idea, anyhow."

"Gee, thanks," Sam said sarcastically.

Becky was too caught up in the party to notice Sam's reaction. "So will you order the pizzas?"

"Sure," Sam said. "Why not?" She noticed a tall kid walking by with an open can of beer. "That kid can't drink in here, Becky."

"Oh, Sam, come on," Becky scoffed. "What's the big deal?"

"Hey, Becky, there isn't any food!" a girl with short blond hair yelled in Becky's ear.

"How about if I go order the pizzas?" Carrie offered.

"Thanks," Sam said with a grin. "Order six, I guess."

Carrie made her way to the phone, passing a half-dozen other kids guzzling beers. It wasn't going to be easy for Sam to stop people from drinking at this party. After Carrie ordered the pizzas, she walked by Ian, who was standing near the stairs with a group of teens who were all older and bigger than he was.

"So, Graham Perry is really your father?" a pretty girl with dark, curly hair was asking.

"Yeah," Ian answered.

"That is so awesome," she breathed. "What's he like?"

Ian shrugged.

"I think he's the greatest musician in the world," she said.

"Yeah, he is. You know, I jam with him a lot," Ian told her.

"For real?" she asked.

"Hey, do they make microphone stands short enough for you?" an older guy asked. Several of the girls guffawed at his joke.

"I don't know," Ian said. "Do they make books dumb enough for you to read?"

This brought a bigger laugh, and Carrie smiled to herself as she made her way back to the family room. Ian seemed to be holding his own.

"So why don't you dance with me?" a tall kid with greasy black hair was asking Sam when Carrie returned.

"Because I'm nineteen and you're sixteen," Sam said.

"I like older women," the kid said. "I bet I could teach you a thing or two," he added with a leer. It was apparent to both Carrie and Sam that the kid had been drinking.

Sam's face took on a look of disgust. "Yeah, in your dreams." She turned around and saw Carrie. "Help me find the twins, will you? Somebody brought a ton of beer to this party and these kids are getting polluted."

After a search through the house, they finally found both Allie and Becky in the backyard, passionately making out with two boys from the country club.

"Uh, hate to disturb you," Sam said, her voice dripping sarcasm.

"Well, then, don't," Becky said with a giggle, throwing her arms even more tightly around the guy's neck.

"Girls, I need to have a word with you," Sam said, not deterred.

"How about if I have a word with you first?" Allie said. "Bye!"

Sam groaned. "I mean it," she said in a steely voice. "Now."

Something in her tone made Becky and Allie turn toward her. "Oh, all right," Becky said with disgust. She turned to the guy she'd been kissing. "Save my place!" she called to him gaily.

Sam, Carrie, and the twins walked to the other side of the yard.

"Listen," Sam said, "Carrie and I saw a lot of kids drinking in there. I promised your dad this wouldn't happen."

"What am I, a mind reader?" Becky asked Sam, her hands on her hips. "How was I supposed to know that kids would bring beer?"

Carrie was close enough to Becky to smell her breath. "You've been drinking, too," Carrie said quietly.

Becky and Allie shared a look of disdain.

"Big, bad deal," Allie said.

Sam took a deep breath. Carrie could tell that she really wanted to strangle them both. "Look, the only reason your dad let you have this party was because I told him that Carrie and I would chaperone."

"You guys are our responsibility," Carrie added.

"If you say *one word* to *anyone* about being our babysitter, I will be completely humiliated *forever*," Becky hissed.

"Yeah," Allie seconded. "No one will ever speak to us again."

"You *told* them they could drink!" Sam realized as she looked at the twins' defiant faces.

43

Becky and Allie had the good grace to be embarrassed.

"Well, we didn't exactly say they *couldn't*," Allie murmured.

"Hey, the pizza's here!" someone yelled from inside the house.

Carrie and Sam made their way to the front door. As Sam counted out the money Carrie was suddenly struck by an idea.

"Just wait right there," Carrie said to Sam. "I'll drive the car up, and you stick the pizzas in the back seat. I'll explain in a minute."

Carrie raced to the car as the party noise escalated behind her. She heard a crash—a lamp falling over, perhaps. She certainly hoped her idea would work. She was sure that Sam's employer would not appreciate having his house trashed.

When Carrie pulled the car up, Sam loaded the pizzas into the back seat as Carrie explained her plan. "I'm driving the food to the beach," Carrie told Sam. "I hope the party will follow."

"Hey, where's she going with the food?" the greasy-haired guy called out.

"To the beach!" Sam said. "We're turning this into a beach party!"

"Cool!" the guy cried, and jumped in the back of Carrie's car.

"Yeah! Skinny-dipping!" another girl screamed as she jumped in after him.

"So far, so good," Carrie said to Sam through the car window. "I'll meet you down at the beach, right by lifeguard stand six." Then she took off.

It wasn't long before a parade of cars, bikes, and motorcycles snaked its way from the Jacobses' house to the beach. Sam found Carrie simultaneously presiding over the pizza and organizing a group to build a fire.

"You are something else," Sam said with admiration as she dropped down beside Carrie in the sand.

"Just call me the Pied Piper," Carrie laughed, licking some pizza sauce off her fingers.

"Now all we have to do is make sure no one drowns," Sam said as two kids hit the water running.

"Actually, I think you'd like to drown Becky and Allie right about now," Carrie said with a laugh.

"Too true," Sam agreed as she headed for the shoreline to act as lifeguard.

Two cute guys got the fire started. Someone showed up with some marshmallows, which some kids started roasting. Unfortunately, the combination of beer, pizza, and marshmallows got to one guy's stomach, and he started heaving into the sand.

"Gross!" a girl yelled. "Go down the beach if you're gonna heave!"

"Whew! The water is great!" Becky yelled as she ran over to the fire. She had on her bra and bikini panties, which were soaked.

Well, at least she didn't strip down to the buff, Carrie thought, remembering her own embarrassing interlude at a skinny-dipping party on the beach the previous summer.

"Want me to roast you a marshmallow?" Ian asked, coming up beside Becky.

Carrie noticed that Ian was both dressed and dry. Evidently, he hadn't gone swimming.

"Okay," Becky said carelessly. "But make sure it's burnt on the outside and gooey on the inside," she ordered.

"You got it," Ian said, eager to do anything for Becky.

Becky plopped down on the sand next to Ian, pulling her T-shirt on over her wet bra. Ian looked at her sideways, trying not to stare too obviously.

"So is it true that you jam with your dad?" Becky asked Ian as the marshmallow slowly roasted in the fire.

"Sure," Ian said, turning the stick.

"Is he full of it?" Becky asked Carrie.

Carrie busied herself finding a stick and spearing a marshmallow on it. She hated to lie; on the other hand, she didn't want to embarrass Ian. Then she remembered a time when she'd actually seen Ian playing the drums in his father's music room while his father noodled around on the piano.

"No, he's not," Carrie finally said. "Ian plays drums and his dad plays the piano. They sound great together," she added truthfully. They *had* sounded great. No one could sound bad playing drums while Graham Perry sang and played the piano.

"That's max," Becky said, accepting the marshmallow from Ian's stick.

"I have my own band, though," Ian said.

"Why don't you just play with your dad's band?" Becky asked.

"I'm the next musical generation," Ian declared expansively. "Remember, I told you and Allie about industrial music?"

"Oh, yeah, how could I forget?" Becky said, rolling her eyes.

"Hey, they laughed at the Beatles. They laughed at Hammer. No way can you create a new musical form without people laughing at you at first," Ian said seriously.

"Well, it sounds totally bogus," Becky said in a bored voice. "Roast me another marshmallow."

Ian took another marshmallow from the bag as Carrie withdrew hers from the fire. Becky really was obnoxious. She felt like smacking her for being so nasty to Ian.

"My band's gigging at the Play Café Thursday," Ian said, "for that underage party. So how about you come and see for yourself?"

"Wow! Your band is going to be at the Play Café?" Becky asked, impressed in spite of herself.

Carrie stared at Ian through the fire. This was the first she had heard about him playing at the Play Café. Was he lying?

"Yeah," Ian said. "So, you gonna come?"

"Okay," Becky said.

Ian's face lit up as he handed Becky the hot marshmallow. Carrie only hoped that Becky was not going to break his heart.

It was well after midnight when the party finally broke up. Sam found one guy so drunk that he'd passed out in the sand—she had to rouse him with a bucket of cold water. Carrie volunteered to drive Becky, Allie, and Ian home, then come back to help Sam with the cleanup.

Meanwhile Sam did her best to insure that none of the drivers was drunk. She knew only too well what the consequences of drunk driving could be.

"I really appreciate this," Sam said half an hour later as Carrie shone the flashlight on the sand so they could see to pick up the trash.

"We're just lucky this party didn't get busted," Carrie said.

"I'm going to kill the twins, I mean it," Sam said, gingerly picking up a half-eaten slice of pizza and tossing it into a plastic garbage bag.

"On the way home they were begging me to ask you not to tell their dad that kids were drinking," Carrie told Sam. "I told them it was up to you."

"No way am I keeping this a secret," Sam said, surveying the beach for more debris. She found an empty beer can and picked it up. "Was I this stupid when I was fourteen?" she asked herself out loud.

"You know, it was funny," Carrie mused. "I was sitting by the fire listening to Becky and Ian talk, and I felt so *old!*"

"Well, fourteen and nineteen are light-years apart," Sam said. She cast one last look around. "I think we got all the garbage."

Carrie stirred the last embers of the fire thoughtfully. "It all gets so much more complicated, doesn't it?" She looked over at Sam. "I decided to say yes to Josh, by the way. He'll be here tomorrow."

"Well, it could be a good move," Sam said, plopping down in the sand next to Carrie. "He could make Billy jealous."

"Oh, Sam, I don't want to play that game!" Carrie cried. "I mean, I know that stuff works for you, but it's just not for me."

"No?" Sam asked with an arched eyebrow. "Can you honestly say that there isn't some part of you that wants to make Billy crazed?"

Carrie didn't answer. She just sighed and made sure the last of the fire was out.

"Brr, I'm freezing," Sam said. "Let's boogie." She pulled Carrie up off the sand and hoisted her garbage bag over her shoulder. "Don't look so bummed, girlfriend," Sam advised as they started toward their cars. "Josh's visit could prove to be quite an interesting adventure!"

"Or the stupidest decision I ever made," Carrie mumbled.

"Or that," Sam agreed cheerfully. "But at least life ain't boring!"

FOUR

Carrie woke up and stretched deliciously. *It's my day off,* she said to herself, *and I'm going to make the most of it. No darling Chloe worrying about whether to wear her red shoes or her blue shoes, no Ian teaching the Zit Men how to play their microwaves better—nothing but fun!*

Of course, there was the little matter of Josh's arrival to deal with, and things were bound to get complicated with Billy. *But I am not going to obsess about this,* Carrie vowed. *I am going to have fun!*

Carrie ran to the window to check out the weather. It was an absolutely gorgeous Maine day, with the morning temperature cool and not a cloud in the breezy sky. Better yet, both Emma and Sam had been able to arrange their work schedules so that all three girls had the whole day free. And

Kurt had made arrangements for Carrie, Billy, Sam, Pres, Emma, and him to go out deep-sea fishing on a friend's charter boat! Carrie had been fishing only once before, off the coast of New Jersey, and she had loved it.

Sam, however, had been a little dubious about the day's activities. "Fishing?" she had asked skeptically. "I don't even order fish at a restaurant, and there you don't have to cook it, much less catch it!"

But Carrie and Emma had convinced her that it would be really fun, and Sam finally said she'd come along.

"Okay, I'll let Pres cut my bait," she joked. The other girls cracked up.

Carrie wasn't due at the marina until noontime—Kurt had told them that it was best to fish on the incoming tide, and high tide was scheduled for four o'clock that afternoon—and Josh wasn't arriving until six o'clock. That meant Carrie could hang out with her friends, spend some time alone with Billy, and still meet Josh's ferry.

Carrie showered and dressed, then bopped downstairs to the small darkroom the Templetons had set up recently. Claudia was getting involved in photography, too, and Graham had set up the darkroom for her as a birthday surprise. Claudia had told Carrie she could use it anytime she wanted.

She had just finished printing a contact sheet when the phone outside the darkroom rang.

"Templeton residence, Carrie speaking," she answered, wiping her hands on her smock.

"Hello, Carrie, it's May Spencer-Rumsey. How are you this glorious day?"

Carrie's heart started pounding. *May Spencer-Rumsey! I didn't really think she'd ever call again. But I have to keep my cool.* Carrie sat down on the floor outside the darkroom before she said anything.

"Just fine, May. It *is* beautiful outside. By the way, Chloe has done nothing for the last twenty-four hours but talk about what a good time she had with Annie. Your granddaughter was a big hit." *There. That's the right thing to say. I think.*

"That's just why I'm calling," May said with genuine warmth in her voice. "Annie has been clamoring for Chloe, too. So do you think that you could bring Chloe over for a play date tomorrow afternoon? If you'd like, you could bring some of your photos of the island at the same time, and we could go through them together."

Bingo! Carrie thought. *I may be screwing up royally with Billy and Josh, but so far so good with my pictures.*

"I would love to come," Carrie said with enthusiasm, "and I know Chloe would as well. I'll just check it out with Claudia Templeton and let you know. Is that all right?"

"Sounds just fine," May agreed.

"I'll call you this evening to confirm," Carrie promised before hanging up. Her heart was pounding in her chest. She was really going to get the chance to show her work to May! *Carrie, old girl*, she told herself, *this just could be the opportunity of a lifetime.*

When Carrie arrived at the marina at eleven-thirty, her five friends were already there.

"Ahoy, girlfriend!" Sam cried out when she saw her. "Hurry on down here, or we're gonna cut you up and use you for bait!" Apparently Sam's attitude about this trip had changed in a hurry.

When Carrie got closer to the boat, which was called the *Gladiola*, she saw why Sam's disposition had improved. Sam's friend Pres had never looked better. He had on an orange University of Tennessee T-shirt and black Lycra biker shorts. On his head he wore a white baseball cap turned backwards.

"Hey, Carrie! Glad to see you!" Billy hugged and kissed her when she arrived. Carrie kissed him back, but an image of Josh flashed through her mind as she did. *Stop this!* she told herself. *Or else you'll ruin the whole trip.*

Billy looked great, too. He was dressed in a blue denim workshirt and a pair of old white Levi's that were ripped at the knees. *He'd look great in anything, even my grandfather's pajamas,* Carrie thought. *I'm going to have to talk to him about Josh sometime today. That'll be a ton of fun. Maybe he'll bring it up.* But somehow she doubted it.

Carrie was wearing warm clothes as Kurt had suggested the day before—jeans and a red-and-blue long-sleeved rugby shirt. Emma had on something similar, except her rugby shirt was from a real British football team and said "Tottenham Hotspur" across the front. Sam, in contrast, was wearing a blue halter top and blue leggings with blue high-tops. She carried a blue denim jacket. "I'm hoping we catch some bluefish," she explained with an impish smile.

After they boarded the *Gladiola* and motored out of the marina, Kurt assembled them all in the stern of the boat. They all knew that he had worked on fishing boats for many years when he was growing up, so they all listened attentively.

"Okay, listen up," he said, all business. "We're going to have fun out here, but we're also going to be careful. Careful about how much beer gets drunk, careful about horseplay on the boat, careful down in the engine room, careful with the equipment. Got it?"

They all nodded. *Wow! This is a side of Kurt I've never seen*, Carrie thought. *He's a real leader.* And Carrie noticed that Emma seemed to be having the same thought.

"Okay!" Kurt said, leaning easily against the railing as spray kicked up from their wake. "If you run into a problem with the equipment, let me, Mike the captain, or Charlie the mate know about it. We'll help you. We each get to keep one fish, and the rest we'll give to Mike to sell. That's why we get to go out for free. Now, let's catch 'em!"

Kurt and Charlie spent the rest of the half-hour ride out to the fishing grounds showing them all how to rig up and use the equipment. They were going to spend the first part of the afternoon jigging for cod, and then troll for bluefish on the way back to the marina.

When they got to the grounds, which were marked by a series of yellow buoys in the water, they all took their rods and reels and let a seven-ounce metal jig shaped like a torpedo drop down to the bottom of the ocean. "Now, when it hits bottom," Kurt explained, "reel up a few turns, and then start lifting and lowering your rod, just like this." Suddenly Kurt's face changed as he realized he already had a bite. "One on! One on!" he called out, and started reeling furiously, his rod bent nearly in two.

The group all gathered around him. Kurt obviously had hooked a big fish on his very first try.

"Here, Emma, take my rod," Kurt said, "You can have the honor of reeling in the first fish."

Emma smiled but refused. "It's your fish to catch or lose, Kurt," she said. "Keep reeling!"

Shortly afterward, Charlie reached down with a gaff hook, which was like a giant fishhook on the end of a long pole, gaffed Kurt's fish, and swung it up into the *Gladiola*.

"Big red cod," Kurt said with a huge grin.

"It's great eating and it matches Sam's hair."
They all cracked up.

"Lemme show you how it's done," Sam retorted. "It's time for me to catch my watery cousin." She dropped her jig to the bottom and started lifting and lowering her rod, as Kurt had shown them.

Within two hours the young crew of the *Gladiola* had hooked and landed twenty-eight cod, with Carrie catching the biggest one—a specimen of about fourteen pounds. Even the captain came down from the bridge to shake her hand when she landed it. "Ayuh, that's a fine fish, young lady," he'd said. Carrie, knowing that real Mainers don't usually have a lot to say, took it as a compliment.

It was nearly time for the run back to the marina when the mate came up on deck with six fishing rods that were set up very differently, with lures that looked like surgical tubing instead of the metal jigs they had been using before. He put each of these rods into a special holder at the stern of the boat, told his passengers to reel up their jigs, and then started letting line off each of the new rods as the *Gladiola* turned for home.

"Hey, those are bluefish rigs, right?" Sam asked excitedly. "We saw some guys surfcasting for bluefish on the beach a few days ago. Looked like fun!"

"These are a little different," Charlie said in his slow, down-easter tones. "But they're for the blues. Hey, did you know I had to shoot my dog the other day?"

"That's awful!" Sam cried, completely horrified. "Was he mad?"

"Ayuh, he wasn't too darned pleased," Charlie said with a twinkle in his eye. They all laughed.

Charlie told them that they would troll as the boat headed slowly back to the marina, and if a bluefish grabbed any of the lures trailing behind the boat, they'd know it. They all decided that Pres, who had caught only two cod, would get a chance at the first bluefish.

"Not much of an ocean in Tennessee," Pres joked. "I hope these fish ain't allergic to li'l ol' me!"

Zing! One of the reels started singing. A bluefish had nailed one of the lures. Pres grabbed the rod and started reeling. "Whoa," he said, "this ain't no little catfish!"

"Hoo-boy! Look at those Tennessee muscles bulge!" Sam said, nudging Carrie in the ribs. But Carrie wasn't paying much attention. *I've got to talk to Billy about Josh,* she thought. *And I'd better do it now.*

While the others gathered around Pres, Carrie moved over toward Billy and kissed him lightly on the neck.

"Hey, that's my kind of bait," Billy said with a laugh.

Carrie smiled somewhat uncomfortably. *Might as well tell him now,* she thought. "Uh, can we go up in the bow and talk for a bit?"

Billy flashed his patented big grin. "Sure thing," he said easily.

The two of them made their way to a small bench in the bow and sat down.

Carrie took Billy's hand. *As if that's going to make it easier,* she thought. She wasn't sure what to say, so she decided to tell Billy the truth.

"Remember yesterday how I said that Josh might come up to the island for a few days?" Carrie said uncomfortably. Billy nodded.

"Well, he's coming this afternoon. I'm picking him up at the ferry at six o'clock."

Billy didn't say anything. Carrie felt more and more uncomfortable as the seconds ticked by.

"Don't you have anything to say about it?" she finally asked him.

Billy stared out toward the rapidly approaching shoreline. Then he turned toward Carrie. "Look," he said, looking her right in the eye, "I feel like you have this script in your mind of what I'm supposed to say to you."

"No, I don't," Carrie protested. "It's just that—"

"I think you do," Billy interrupted quietly. "Anyway, that's how it feels." He looked out at the water. "Am I happy that he's coming? No, not really. It means I probably won't get to see you for a few days, until he's gone, right?"

"I guess so," Carrie agreed in a low voice.

"Right," Billy said, "so that's a drag. But am I going to pitch a fit over it, as my friend Pres would say? No way, Carrie, not a chance. Hey, have fun with him," he concluded.

He doesn't love me, he doesn't love me, a horrible voice cried in Carrie's heart. *He could never say that to me if he really loved me. I don't know what to say or do now.*

"Well, okay," Carrie managed, trying not to let her voice quaver. She desperately wanted Billy not to know how hurt she felt.

"Just so I know how you feel, and, um . . ."

"Hey, don't sweat it," Billy said. "I've been in this situation before. Let's go back and see what Pres has caught."

And before Carrie could say anything else, Billy was on his way back to the stern, leaving Carrie behind. *I've really blown it*, Carrie said to herself. *I've ruined everything*.

She stared out at the sea as they headed for shore, trying to figure out where she'd gone so wrong.

It was almost six o'clock, and Carrie was sitting on one of the park benches on the grass near where the Sunset Island ferry pulled in. Her friends had gone on an expedition to Rubie's restaurant, where Kurt had arranged for Rubie herself to cook their fish right on the spot. Carrie had stayed behind to meet Josh. In spite of her anxiety about Billy, she was really looking forward to seeing Josh. Carrie sighed and kept a lookout for the ferry. Her feelings really made no sense at all!

A few minutes later, the ferry pulled into its slip with a thud. And there was Josh! He was practically the first one off the boat.

Josh looked as cute as ever. His hair was

longer and fell over his eye in a sexy wave. He was wearing faded jeans, a Yale T-shirt, and black Ray-Ban sunglasses. Carrie's heart leaped as he approached. *Hey, I'm actually really glad to see him!*

"Hey, cutie," Josh said, taking Carrie in his arms. "You look great, and you feel great," he said softly.

Carrie hugged him back enthusiastically. "I'm really happy to see you, Josh," she said, squeezing him lovingly. "We're going to have a great time. Everyone's looking forward to meeting you," she said automatically.

Oops. Well, almost everyone, Carrie thought ruefully.

"Great!" Josh said. "When does the fun begin?"

"Now. We're going to have a blast," Carrie replied, and they walked hand in hand toward the car.

As Carrie drove toward the Templetons' house (where Claudia had very kindly said that Josh was welcome as a guest), Josh kept up a running monologue about his summer job and everyone back home in New Jersey.

As the car turned a corner near the Play Café, Carrie saw Willie Windsor, a friend of the Flirts, walking toward the café with a bunch of kids. That made her think about Billy and how easy it would be to run into him while she was with Josh. *Not that Billy cares*, Carrie thought bitterly.

"I've missed you so much," Josh said, gently putting his hand on Carrie's knee. Carrie stopped at the light and smiled at his loving and oh-so-familiar face. Now here was a guy who truly loved her and wasn't afraid to put it on the line. That was worth a lot.

Maybe she was just too busy being dazzled by Billy Sampson to appreciate what she already had.

FIVE

Carrie gave herself one last look in the mirror and tucked her embroidered white cotton shirt more evenly into her jeans. It was the next day, and she was getting ready to take Chloe—not to mention her photographs—over to May Spencer-Rumsey's. It was funny—the first time she'd gone over there she hadn't given her outfit a second thought, but now she wanted to make sure she made the right impression.

"You look like a talented young photographer," she assured her image in the mirror. *I hope*, she added in her mind as she picked up her portfolio of photographs from the dresser.

Carrie went downstairs and out to the pool in the back, where Claudia, Graham, Josh, and some other friends were lolling in the sun. Carrie marveled again at how gorgeous the new pool was. Construction had just been completed on it the previous week. Chloe seemed to prefer going to the country club to swim with her friends, but it gave Graham an opportunity to swim without any fans gawking at him.

"I'm all ready!" Chloe cried exuberantly, skipping over to Carrie.

She'd helped Chloe dress before she'd dressed herself, and she had to smile again at what the little girl had insisted she wear. Chloe said that Annie's favorite color was pink, so Chloe had chosen a pink denim skirt, a pink T-shirt, pink socks, and a huge pink hair ribbon.

"You look scrumptious," Carrie said, hugging Chloe.

"What's that mean?" Chloe asked, scrunching up her face.

"It means you look delicious, like a strawberry ice-cream cone," Carrie said with a laugh as she straightened Chloe's hair ribbon.

"I don't look like ice cream, I look like a little girl," Chloe said reasonably.

Claudia overheard her daughter and chuckled. "She's very logical. She gets it from my side of the family."

Josh got up from his chaise longue and

came over to Carrie. "You look great," he told her with a grin.

"Maybe I should have dressed up more or something," Carrie said nervously, looking down at herself.

"Relax!" Josh advised. "It isn't like this is a job interview with her in New York. You're neighbors here on Fantasy Island— that makes it completely different."

"Right," Carrie agreed. "Listen, thanks for understanding about my going over there and everything. I just didn't feel right asking if I could bring you."

"I'll just suffer, hanging out here at the pool with a famous rock star," Josh said with a sigh.

"You couldn't care less about him being famous and I know it," Carrie said in a low voice. She knew Josh was completely unimpressed by rock fame; he listened strictly to jazz.

"Hey, he's an interesting guy," Josh said with a shrug. "And he and Claudia are certainly being nice to me."

"I heard that!" Claudia called playfully from her chaise longue. "Keep talking! I love compliments!"

"Hey, Car, knock her dead!" Graham

called from the pool, where he was swimming laps.

Carrie grinned at them all. They were so great to her.

"Well, bye," she told Josh, kissing him lightly on the lips.

He held up crossed fingers. "I'm rooting for you!"

Chloe chattered away as Carrie drove to Ms. Spencer-Rumsey's mansion on the peninsula. "And we're gonna play Barbies and tea party and school," Chloe told Carrie.

"That's great, honey," Carrie said as she pulled the car into the circular drive.

The same young man as last time came out to park the Mercedes. May Spencer-Rumsey greeted them at the front door, Annie right beside her. Both the grandmother and the granddaughter had on jeans, which made Carrie sigh with relief that she'd dressed correctly.

Their outfits weren't such a hit with Chloe, though. She scrutinized her friend, then looked up at Carrie. "I want to go home and put on jeans," she told her au pair.

"You look fine, sweetie," Carrie assured the little girl.

"I want jeans!" Chloe insisted. She looked as if she was ready to cry.

"You can wear some of mine, right, Grandma?" Annie asked her grandmother.

"Absolutely," May agreed. "Take Chloe up and get her outfitted." The two little girls skipped happily upstairs.

"Well, thank you for that," Carrie said with a sheepish grin. "You just averted play-date disaster."

May laughed. "Oh, I know what it's like to feel as if you haven't dressed appropriately," she said easily, leading Carrie into the kitchen. "Children are much more sensitive to such things than we imagine."

A sturdy-looking woman in a black-and-white uniform, her blond hair in a tight bun, was just putting some cookies in the oven.

"Elise, we'll have tea out in the gazebo, please," May told the woman. "Hot or cold?" she asked Carrie.

"Either is fine," Carrie answered.

"Bring both," May told the woman, who nodded agreeably.

"Elise had her day off the last time you were here," May said companionably as she led Carrie out back to the gazebo. "She's the world's most fabulous cook, a fact my waistline can attest to."

The last time that Carrie had been at the house she hadn't been out back, but she had seen a breathtaking view from the picture window. This time, Carrie walked out to the round, weathered wooden gazebo that was perched precariously at the top of a low, rocky cliff. Waves crashed on the boulders below. The magnificence of it took Carrie's breath away.

"It is incredible, isn't it?" May said as if she could read Carrie's mind.

Carrie nodded. The warm sun beat down on her head and the salt spray tickled her nose. "The beauty of this island is just so . . . so . . . " Carrie faltered, at a loss for words.

"I know the feeling," May said kindly. "I can't describe it adequately with words, either. I think pictures will tell the story so much more fully." May looked meaningfully at the portfolio that Carrie clutched in her hand. "May I?" she asked.

Mutely Carrie handed over her photos and sat on the hand-carved wooden chair behind May. Her heart beat rapidly in her chest. Her photography was so personal to her—it was very difficult to sit there, waiting to be judged.

It seemed forever that May looked through Carrie's shots, without uttering so much as a syllable. Elise came and went with the tea, which sat untouched on a silver tray before them. Finally, May looked up at Carrie, put down the photos, and poured them both glasses of iced tea before speaking.

"Fabulous," she said simply, handing Carrie the tea.

"Pardon me?" Carrie said. She didn't even reach to take the tea from May's hand, so taken aback was she at this assessment.

"They're fabulous," May repeated. "Drink your tea," she added with a laugh. "I think your tongue must be sticking to the roof of your mouth."

Carrie obediently put the tea to her lips. "You . . . you really think . . . ?"

"I really think," May said, nodding at Carrie. "You've captured something very special in your shots, Carrie. You're a very, very talented young woman."

"Thank you," Carrie said earnestly. "That means so much to me, coming from you."

"These are among the best photographs I've ever seen of the island," May said. "And believe me, I have absolutely no reason to butter you up—I'm not that kind of person." May drank her tea thirstily and bit into a tiny cucumber sandwich. "I'd very much like to work with you on a book of photographs of the island."

Carrie practically choked on her iced tea. May Spencer-Rumsey actually wanted her photos for a book? "I . . . I don't know what to say . . ."

"Say yes!" May said, laughing, "and we can get to work!"

"Yes!" Carrie cried happily.

"Wonderful," May said. "You must try some paté—Elise makes it herself," she said, spreading some on a cracker.

Carrie had absolutely no appetite, but she obligingly crunched the cracker in her mouth.

"We'll need a simple contract," May mused. "Have you an agent?"

"Uh, I could get one," Carrie said in a small voice. "Or maybe a lawyer could do it?" Perhaps Jane Hewitt, Emma's employer, would help her.

"Certainly. Anyway, it's just a technicality," May said. "Have him or her contact me. Now, how many more photos of the island do you have?"

"Tons," Carrie admitted. "I just selected a few to bring you. I thought these were the best."

"I want to see them all," May said firmly.

"I may see something in a shot that you don't see."

"All right," Carrie agreed.

"Let's meet the day after tomorrow," May suggested. "Around one? And I'll have a contract for you to give to your lawyer."

"I'll need to arrange the time off with Claudia," Carrie said, "but I'm sure she'll say it's fine."

"Well, then, here's to our artistic venture!" May said, lifting her glass of iced tea to clink it against Carrie's.

"I can't thank you enough," Carrie said.

"You are an artist," May said simply. "I should be thanking you."

"She liked them! She liked my work!" Carrie cried as she ran back to the pool behind the Templetons' house.

"That's my girl!" Josh crowed, hugging her exuberantly.

"So, tell us more!" Claudia demanded. She was flipping burgers on a small grill, wearing an apron over a tiny bikini.

"She's going to publish them in a book about Sunset Island!" Carrie whooped. "Can you believe it?"

"Get down, girl!" Graham crowed from the pool, where he was playing tag with Ian.

"Hey, Daddy, I want to swim with you," Chloe said.

"Go get changed and come on in!" he cried.

"Come on, Chloe, I'll help you get into your suit," Carrie said.

"I can do it without help," Chloe said. "Annie doesn't need help. I'll go up by myself." She turned and walked into the house.

"Well, she's turning into quite the independent little cuss." Graham chuckled. "Soon she'll be babysitting *you*, Carrie!"

"Come on, tell us all about what happened," Josh said, making room on his chaise for Carrie.

Carrie related the entire story. "So that's it," she concluded. "She wants to meet with me the day after tomorrow at one to look at the rest of my shots. That is, if it's okay with you," she added hastily to Claudia.

"Fine," Claudia said, checking the burgers. "I'm doing a charity mother-daughter fashion show with Chloe that afternoon, anyway."

"Wow, Carrie, you're gonna be famous!" Ian called from the pool. "Of course, so will I," he added, "once industrial music really catches on."

"Anybody home?" a voice called from the

side of the house. Becky Jacobs popped her head around the corner. She was wearing a tiny white crop top that bared her stomach, and a pair of teeny-tiny white shorts. Her hair was held back by a wide white headband. She looked at least eighteen years old.

"Becky!" Ian cried, evidently shocked to see her. It appeared to Carrie that he tried to stand up taller in the pool, but even so he barely came up to his father's shoulder.

"I was in the neighborhood," Becky said carelessly.

"If you consider the entire island the neighborhood," Sam commented, coming up behind Becky. "Hi, all. Sorry for not calling. Becky insisted."

"Oh, that's cool," Ian said, trying to sound nonchalant. He got out of the pool. "Want to stay for burgers?"

"Sure," Becky said, sitting down on the nearest chaise. "Hi, Graham," she called to Ian's father in the pool.

"Hi, Becky," Graham said, a smile playing at his lips.

Claudia shot Carrie a significant look. Carrie could tell that Claudia, too, was hoping that Becky wasn't paying attention to Ian just to be near his famous father.

"Who are you?" Becky asked Josh.

"Honestly, you have the world's worst manners," Sam chided her.

"I'm just asking a question," Becky said. "What am I supposed to do, ignore a cute guy I don't know?"

"I'm Josh," Josh said easily. "Carrie's boyfriend."

"Time out," Becky said, looking from Josh to Carrie and back to Josh. "What about—"

"How do you want your burger, Becky?" Claudia asked loudly, interrupting Becky. It was only too clear that Becky was going to ask about Billy and embarrass everyone.

"Medium," Becky answered. She examined Carrie thoughtfully. "Wow, you're a lot wilder than you look."

"Thanks," Carrie said ironically.

Ian looked Becky over shyly. "Want to swim? But I guess you can't swim in that."

"Sure I can," Becky said flippantly. "But it might get see-through when it's wet." Ian gulped hard at that thought while Becky pulled the white headband off her hair. "Last one in is a rotten egg!" she yelled, and jumped into the pool.

"I think I'll cool off, too," Josh said quietly. Evidently Becky's almost-mention of Billy hadn't been lost on him. He did a perfect dive into the deep end. Ian followed with a belly-flop.

Carrie took the platter of burgers from Claudia and carried it over to the picnic table. Sam followed and sat down, straddling a bench. "Sorry about Becky's big mouth," Sam said.

"Oh, it's okay," Carrie sighed. "It's not like Josh doesn't know about Billy. It's just awkward, that's all."

"Yeah, I can imagine," Sam agreed, reaching for a handful of potato chips from the table. "So what happened at your big meeting with Madam Moneybags?" she asked. "Did she like your photos?"

Carrie put down the cole slaw she was carrying. Her face lit up. "She loved them. She wants to use them in a book about the island!"

"Way to go, girl!" Sam cheered. "That is so cool!"

"I know," Carrie agreed happily. "I can hardly believe it."

"Wait until you tell everyone tonight," Sam said. "We've got to celebrate!"

Carrie, Sam, and Emma were going out that night with Josh, Pres, and Kurt. They'd talked about going to the movies, or maybe just going for a ride out to the dunes if the weather was good. It had been Sam's idea. Carrie was uncomfortable with the whole plan, especially since Pres and Billy were best friends and roommates. But Emma and Sam had talked her into it.

"You're sure this is going to be okay tonight?" Carrie asked, watching Josh frolic in the pool.

"Totally," Sam assured her. "Pres is a sophisticated guy. Besides, it's not like you lied to anyone about anything."

"That's true," Carrie conceded.

"Anyway, from what you've told me about Billy's reaction to this whole thing, having Pres relay the details of your date with Josh might be a really good thing," Sam pronounced.

"He wouldn't say anything, would he?" Carrie asked.

"Why, are you planning to jump Josh's bones in front of us tonight or something?"

"No, of course not," Carrie said, setting down a platter of hamburger buns.

"Then not to worry," Sam said with a shrug.

"Dinner!" Claudia called as she and Carrie brought the last of the food to the table.

"We really didn't mean to barge in for dinner," Sam told Claudia. "We can leave."

"Oh, it's fine," Claudia assured her. "And I know Ian is happy," she added with a smile.

The swimmers dried off and everyone helped themselves from the overflowing buffet. Chloe finally made her entrance in her favorite yellow bathing suit, her inflatable duck already around her middle.

"I was just about ready to come check on you," Claudia told her daughter.

"Hey, what about swimming?" Chloe demanded.

"We're eating now, honey," Claudia said.

"Okay, then I'll swim after," Chloe decided, scrambling to sit next to Carrie at the table.

"Ian told me his band is playing at the Play Café this Thursday," Becky told Graham. "Will you be there?"

Ian looked hopefully over at his father. "Sure," Graham said. "If Ian wants me to come."

"Yeah, that would be cool," Ian said, trying not to sound too excited.

"Great," Becky said. "I'll be there, too." She took a bite of her burger before speaking. "You really need a hipper look, Ian. No offense, but those black pants and that pink shirt you wore to my party were really bogus."

"But that's my stage outfit!" Ian protested.

"Yeah, so you said." Becky sighed. "Listen, I'm willing to help. How about if we go shopping tomorrow?"

Ian's face lit up. "You and me?"

Becky nodded coolly.

It was obvious that Ian could hardly contain his happiness. Becky had just asked him on a shopping date!

"Where should we go?" Ian inquired.

"How about that new store next door to the Cheap Boutique?" Becky suggested.

"Cheap Charlie's?" Ian asked eagerly.

"Yeah, that's it," Becky agreed. "I hear it's pretty hip."

"We could ride our bikes over," Ian suggested.

Becky looked at him as if he were eating dead bugs. "No way am I going to be seen on a bike, okay?"

"Oh, yeah, well . . ." Ian stammered, realizing his mistake.

"Sam will drive us. Won't you, Sam?" Becky asked sweetly.

"Not tomorrow, babe," Sam said, slathering mustard on her second burger. "I'm taking Allie horseback riding."

"I'll take you," Carrie offered.

"You won't actually come in, though, right?" Becky asked Carrie.

"No, I won't," Carrie assured her. "I'll drop you guys off and show Josh some of the stores on the bay side."

"Oh, did you want to come along, Graham?" Becky asked, her eyes wide.

"Sorry, Becky, Graham and I have plans," Claudia said, trying not to laugh at Becky's audacity.

"Oh well, another time," Becky said with a shrug.

"Are you and Becky going on a date?" Chloe asked Ian loudly.

"We're just . . . hanging out," Ian said, looking sideways at Becky.

"Well, if Josh is Carrie's boyfriend, and Ian is Becky's boyfriend, I need a boyfriend, too," Chloe reasoned.

"Maybe you can have Billy," Becky said, sipping her Coke. "I hear he's free."

There was silence at the table.

"Once a monster, always a monster," Sam said, trying to lighten the mood.

Becky looked from Josh to Carrie and realized from the expressions on their faces that she'd gone too far. "Hey, it was a joke!" she protested weakly.

But nobody was laughing.

SIX

"On the national weather radar map, Tropical Storm Julius continues to churn in the western Caribbean and is expected to be upgraded to a hurricane by tonight. Forecasters expect it to make landfall somewhere on the Florida coast in two days. The local Maine forecast calls for continued sunny skies—"

Carrie reached over and snapped off the car radio. *Ah, sweet silence*, she thought. *I deserve it.* She rolled the car window down all the way and let the breeze waft the smell of the Atlantic Ocean to her nostrils.

Carrie was on her way to meet Kurt, who had promised her the day before to take her on a photography expedition. "I'll show you a side of Sunset Island you've never imagined!" he said with a strange look in his eyes.

Carrie had agreed enthusiastically to go with him, and said she'd excuse herself from Josh for a couple of hours. She'd left feeling a little guilty for leaving Josh yet again to go off by herself. But he had been really nice about it and said he wanted to finish the book he was reading.

The triple date the night before had gone fine, too. Josh fit right in with her friends, and Pres was as nice as he could be. In fact, it didn't seem to bother anybody that she was with Josh instead of Billy. *Anybody but me, that is*, she added ruefully to herself.

Claudia had been great about her taking a few hours off, too. Carrie had explained to her that Kurt was going to show her some special parts of the island, and that she wanted to get the photos for May Spencer-Rumsey. Claudia had agreed, and had even offered to take care of Chloe that evening so that Carrie could develop her shots in the darkroom.

She pulled into the driveway of the Ackerman family's modest home on the bay side of the island, where Kurt was waiting for her.

"Hey, Carrie, how are you doing?" he shouted as she pulled up.

"Great," Carrie said, jumping out of the car. "I really appreciate your doing this for me."

"Hey, my pleasure," Kurt said. "Like I always say, there's much more to this island than the tourists see, and I'm the guy to show it to you." Kurt cocked his head in the direction of an old Jeep that sat in the driveway. "I borrowed a Jeep from one of Rubie's friends. Some of the places we're going could be a little rough on the Templetons' Mercedes."

Carrie unloaded her camera equipment from the Mercedes and put it in the Jeep. "Buckle up," Kurt said with a smile. "I can't have you bouncing out when we hit a bump. First stop, the year 1863."

"Eighteen sixty-three?" Carrie asked, genuinely confused, as Kurt pulled out of the driveway.

"Yep," Kurt said. "We're going back in time. Hang on!"

He abruptly turned the Jeep off the main road onto a rutted, grassy track. He guided the car expertly for about a mile, up hills, down hills, finally reaching a point where the track looked like no one had driven on it in years. Carrie was mightily impressed. Suddenly, Kurt shut off the engine.

"Take out your camera. We're here," he said.

"We're where?" Carrie asked.

"Like I said, 1863!" Kurt laughed, climbing out of the Jeep. "It's the middle of the Civil War, and President Lincoln is afraid that Confederate frigates are going to steam right past Sunset Island and straight into Portland harbor."

Carrie was completely baffled. *What in the world is he talking about?* she thought as she followed Kurt up one of the dunes.

On the other side of the dune she saw a wondrous sight: carved into the bluffs were huge stone gun emplacements, some with piles of cannonballs still next to them! Each one commanded a view of the entire bay approach to the city of Portland.

"Pretty nifty, huh, Carrie?" Kurt asked with a smile as he hunkered down in one of the bunkers.

"Amazing," Carrie agreed as she fired off photo after photo of the gun emplacements. "It's like a time warp here. Did these cannons ever get fired?"

"Only in someone's imagination." Kurt laughed. "The Confederate navy never made it up this far. Come on. If you're through, I'll continue the grand tour."

Kurt and Carrie walked back to the Jeep. They piled in and Kurt cut directly across some hills instead of heading back along the track. *He knows this island like the back of his hand*, Carrie marveled.

"Where'd you learn so much about the Civil War?" Carrie shouted over the roar of the Jeep.

"One of my uncles taught me. He's into the history of this island big time. Says it makes him appreciate it more. Guess he's right," Kurt shouted back, both hands firmly gripping the wheel.

"Ready for stop number two?" he continued.

"You bet!" Carrie said as the Jeep slowed to a halt.

"So follow me. And bring your telephoto lens," Kurt advised.

They'd stopped just at the edge of a swampy area. Kurt plunged into the tall bulrushes, and Carrie followed carefully.

"Look!" Kurt whispered, taking Carrie's arm and pointing across a small pond.

Sitting in the branches of a small tree was the biggest bird that Carrie had ever seen in her life. *It's the size of a small child!* she thought, amazed.

"What kind of bird is that?" she whispered as quietly as she could, not wanting to scare it.

"It's a great blue heron," Kurt whispered back. "It has a wingspan of about five feet. Want to photograph it?"

"And how!" Carrie said.

"Okay, then, here's the plan. I'm going to toss a rock into the pond, which should startle the bird. It's going to take off just when the rock hits the water. You snap the picture just as it takes flight. Got it?"

"Got it. Ready when you are," Carrie murmured softly. She engaged her camera's motorized film winder and adjusted her telephoto lens. She felt sure she could get some great closeups.

Kurt leaned over, picked up a small rock, and launched it toward the center of the pond. *Splash!* The rock hit. The heron, startled, took flight.

Whirrrrrr! Carrie snapped off photos every quarter of a second. "These are going to be awesome!" Carrie cried out. "The light's just perfect here."

"Glad to be of service to you and my island." Kurt bowed modestly. "Ready for the last stop on this leg of the tour?"

"Let's go!" Carrie said. She felt ready for anything.

"This is going to be a little different," Kurt warned her as they walked back to the Jeep. "But it's an important part of life on this island."

They got in the Jeep, and this time Kurt drove back toward town on the main road. But instead of following Shore Road right into the downtown area, he turned left about a mile before Main Street and followed a winding, unpaved lane that seemed to be heading out toward the ocean. Carrie saw that the lane had no street sign.

"What road is this?" Carrie asked.

"It doesn't have a name," Kurt replied grimly. "A lot of the people who summer on this island would prefer that it didn't exist at all."

Kurt slowed the Jeep as they pulled up into a small cluster of shacks, rusted-out automobiles, and broken-down household appliances. Clothing hung out on clotheslines made it obvious that people lived here. *Good grief*, Carrie thought, *it looks like something out of* The Grapes of Wrath! *This isn't glorious, romantic Sunset Island. This is a poverty zone.*

"Welcome to the other side of Sunset Island," Kurt said tersely.

Carrie was horrified. "Who lives here?"

"Lots of people," Kurt said, getting out of the Jeep. "Just not people the tourists want to acknowledge."

"I can't believe I've spent so much time on this island without knowing this part of it existed," Carrie began.

"Makes my neighborhood look rich, huh?" Kurt said. "These people are dirt-poor. They have no place to go, no future. And no one seems to care."

Carrie assembled her equipment and climbed out after him. *It's my responsibility to take pictures of this,* she thought. *It may not be pretty, and some people might not want to look at it, but real photojournalists tell the whole story, and I'm going to be a real photojournalist.*

She started shooting pictures of everything she saw. A hungry-looking stray cat. A two-year-old girl with a dirty face and distended belly. A broken-down old pickup truck resting on four flat tires. An outhouse, its door hanging partially off its hinges. A fetid-looking swamp where mosquitoes and flies swarmed over a dead animal. The swamp was not fifty feet from a shanty where a little boy with sad eyes sat silently on the front porch.

Carrie ran through her last three rolls of film. *It breaks my heart to see this,* she thought. *So much poverty on such a rich island.* Kurt waited for her in the Jeep, watching her silently.

When Carrie was done, she went back to the Jeep and got in. Without a word, Kurt turned the car around and they drove back to the main road.

Carrie spoke first. "Kurt, I want to thank you for taking me there. I want everyone on this island to see those pictures I just took."

Kurt smiled a little. "I don't take many people down that lane, and you can see why. If you really want everyone to see those pictures, I want to take you now to Rubie's Café. There's someone there I'd like you to meet."

Carrie nodded in agreement. She still had plenty of time to get back to the Templetons'.

Kurt drove them to Rubie's, which Carrie knew was a fish restaurant that was run by Kurt's friend of the same name. He referred to her as his adoptive mom. Emma had told her that she'd eaten codfish there with Kurt on their very first date, and that it was the best fish she'd ever tasted. Coming from Emma, who had dined in the most exclusive restaurants in the world, that was quite a compliment.

Kurt pulled into the small parking lot outside the eatery. The two of them got out and went inside, where Rubie greeted Kurt with her usual bear hug.

When Kurt good-naturedly disengaged himself from Rubie's mammoth embrace, he introduced Carrie to her.

"This is Carrie Alden, a really good friend of mine," he said. "I've been out showing her some interesting places to photograph."

A woman's voice piped up from a table in the corner. "Did you take her out to the fortifications? Did you tell her those fortifications will probably be gone if those developers get their way?"

"Hush, Jade," Rubie said to the raven-haired woman who spoke. "Carrie here isn't much interested in our local politics. Can I get you a glass of iced tea?" she asked Carrie.

"Thank you very much," Carrie replied,

"but I *am* interested in what she's talking about." Carrie walked over to the woman's table. "What developers?"

"I was hoping this topic would come up," Kurt said to Carrie with a smile. "I want to introduce you to Jade Meader, Rubie's older sister. Jade runs a group here called COPE. Jade, meet Carrie Alden."

Carrie shook hands warmly with the woman. Jade looked to be in her seventies, maybe even older. Her black hair was piled high on her head and laugh lines were etched into her weathered skin. All in all, Carrie thought her quite beautiful. "What's COPE?" she asked Jade.

"COPE stands for Citizens of Positive Ethics," Jade explained. "It's a local group that's trying to stop these developers from buying up the land around the fortifications and turning it into a condominium complex." Her voice held a strong note of disgust.

"That would be terrible!" Carrie cried.

"I agree," Jade said firmly. "We're also trying to get some funding to the poor folk on this island, some kind of retraining program for the lobstermen, a health clinic, lots of things. So far, we're not exactly succeeding," she said ruefully. "Why don't you two sit down?"

Carrie and Kurt sat down, and Rubie brought them each a tall glass of iced tea.

"Those fortifications are magnificent!" Carrie said with conviction. "Aren't they a national monument or something?"

"Hardly." Jade laughed, sipping her own tea. "Many folks around here think they're nothing but a ruin. And some of them are looking to get rich quick. So COPE is trying to convince the county government to re-zone the land to protect it."

"Kurt also took me down near the swamp," Carrie said quietly. "I had no idea that kind of poverty existed here. It looks like a Third World country."

"They get about as much respect, too," Jade said. "Those families have been on this island a mighty long time. Yet the rich tourists act like they invented this place!"

"But most of them don't even know about the poverty," Carrie said earnestly. "At least I don't think they do. I mean, I've never heard anyone mention it!"

"Believe me," Jade said in a steely voice, "it is not in rich folks' interest to make known either our national-landmark cause or our poor-folks cause. Everyone just sweeps us under the rug—or tries to, anyway."

"How's it been going lately?" Carrie asked.

"Not bad, not good," Kurt replied for Jade. "The national monument thing is mostly a wintertime issue. The developers tend to lay low during the summer. But if they acquire that land, this time next year there'll be For Sale signs on condos all over that area," Kurt promised grimly.

"Well, I think that area is beautiful and deserves to be protected," Carrie said. "It's history!"

"I think you're right," Rubie called from across the dining room. "But sometimes politicians have a hard time paying attention to history."

"And something has got to be done to help those people," Carrie said fervently, remembering what she'd seen. "Surely if the wealthy people on the island really knew about it, they'd want to help!"

Kurt shook his head sadly. "That may be how you wish the world was, Carrie, but that doesn't make it so."

* * *

When Carrie got back to the Templetons' late that afternoon, her head was swimming. *There's so much going on on this island that no one knows about!* she thought. *Wait till I tell Emma and Sam!*

Carrie went inside and headed upstairs. Claudia was bathing Chloe.

"Hi. Where's Josh?" Carrie asked.

"Oh, he said he was going to be back in a couple of hours. He wanted to take a walk on the beach alone," Claudia replied, rinsing soap off Chloe's face.

"Is it okay if I spend an hour or so in the darkroom?" Carrie asked, praying the answer would be yes.

"Sure," Claudia said. "I told you that before you left, remember?"

"I know," Carrie said, "but I feel guilty, like I'm not doing my job or something."

Claudia laughed. "Carrie, sometimes you are too good to be true. If it makes you feel any better, I'll need you in the kitchen later on. Okay?"

"Sure," Carrie agreed. "And thanks."

Carrie fairly bolted down the stairs to the darkroom, stopping only to pick up the five rolls of film she had shot that afternoon with Kurt. When she emerged an hour and fifteen minutes later, she had contact sheets finished for each of the rolls, and two large prints completed—one of the two-year-old girl with the dirty face, and one of the sad-faced little boy on the porch near the fetid swamp.

The photos broke her heart, but she knew they were really good. *Wait until May sees these*, she thought excitedly.

"Carrie!" Claudia's voice broke into her reverie. "Can you come give me a hand getting dinner together?"

"Coming!" Carrie replied, closing the darkroom door. She felt this had been an extremely productive day. Her head was filled with everything she'd seen and heard. For once, she wasn't worrying about Josh or Billy at all.

Josh got back just in time to have dinner with Carrie and the Templetons, and Carrie spent the entire dinner talking about her afternoon expedition and her discussion with Rubie and Jade.

After dinner was over and the kitchen had been cleaned up, Carrie put Chloe to bed, and then suggested to Josh that the two of them go down to the Play Café to shoot pool.

I doubt that Billy will be there, Carrie said to herself. *And even if he is, I don't care!* For some reason, she felt like throwing caution to the wind. Maybe seeing the things she'd seen that day just put her worries more in perspective.

Josh thought this was a great idea—he and Carrie used to play pool together all the time in the Aldens' basement when they were in high school.

Carrie changed into an oversized white T-shirt with a huge photograph of the jazz musician John Coltrane on it—it was Josh's favorite T-shirt—and a pair of black leggings. When she came downstairs, she saw that Josh had put on an old, faded pair of blue jeans and a black collarless cotton shirt. *He looks really hot in that outfit*, Carrie thought.

They drove the Templetons' Mercedes down to the Play Café. The popular club was packed. Both pool tables were occupied, so after Josh parked himself at a small table to wait, Carrie went off looking for Emma and Sam. They were nowhere to be found, but a small, bespectacled guy did come up to her. It was Howie Lawrence, who had a huge crush on her.

"*Hola*, Carrie! Long time no see," Howie said with a big smile on his face.

Carrie genuinely liked Howie, but sometimes he didn't exactly understand that Carrie was interested in him only as a friend.

"Howie!" Carrie responded warmly. "I'm so glad to see you here. Listen, I want you to come meet a really good friend of mine."

"Great!" Howie said. "I'll follow you anywhere!"

Carrie led Howie back to the table where Josh was waiting. She saw a glimmer of dismay pass across Howie's eyes.

"Howie Lawrence," Carrie said, "this is my boyfriend from home, Josh Lewis. Josh, this is Howie Lawrence, who gives the best parties on the island, and who is a mean pool player, too."

"Cool!" Josh said, standing up to shake Howie's hand. "Want to go a game? I think one of the tables just opened up."

"Uh, no thanks," Howie replied, looking uncomfortable. "I think some people are waiting for me over there," he continued, indicating the far side of the Play Café. "Nice to have met you."

Howie left, shaking his head miserably.

"What was that all about?" Josh asked, taking Carrie's hand.

"Oh, nothing," Carrie replied with a smile. "I think he was afraid you might beat him at pool."

Josh laughed. "I think *you're* afraid I might beat *you*. Why don't you go put our names on the board for the next table?"

"Okay," Carrie said, standing up. "But if I win, you have to do anything I want," she challenged laughingly.

"My pleasure," Josh said, his face lighting up.

Carrie made her way over to the far pool table. *I shouldn't have said that*, she told herself. *I shouldn't flirt with him unless I'm sure my feelings for him are romantic and not just friendly.*

Carrie was writing her name on the blackboard in big letters when she heard a familiar male voice behind her.

"So there I was, reeling in as hard as I could, and the fishing pole was bent over practically in two!"

"Well, I wish you had called me that night. I give great massages for sore muscles," a seductive female voice responded.

Carrie turned around to see who was

talking. Sitting not fifteen feet away, talking, laughing, and gazing into each other's eyes, were none other than Billy Sampson and the girl who the summer before had stolen Kurt from Emma— and then dumped him—Diana De Witt.

SEVEN

Carrie pulled into May Spencer-Rumsey's long driveway precisely at one o'clock, as the two of them had arranged a couple of days earlier. Since May had asked Carrie to bring along all the photos and slides she had ever taken of Sunset Island, Carrie had two big boxes filled with material in the back seat of the car. *I hope she has enough patience to go through them all,* she thought.

As Carrie splashed through a puddle left over from a midmorning thunderstorm, her thoughts momentarily drifted back to an early-morning phone call she had made to her grandmother, who lived in a condo on Florida's eastern coast. Carrie had seen on the TV news that Hurricane Julius was veering north, away from Florida and toward the Carolinas, but she had still wanted to make sure that her grandmother was okay.

"It's that stupid Hurricane Julius," her grandmother growled, "interfering with my morning swim. I can see ten to fifteen-foot waves on the Atlantic from my window."

Carrie had laughed and teased her about taking up bodysurfing.

"Carrie Alden! Welcome back!" May Spencer-Rumsey's voice roused Carrie from her reverie.

"Hi, May," Carrie answered as she climbed out of the Mercedes and took the boxes out of the back. "I've brought every single picture I've ever taken of the island—I hope it's not too much."

"The more you have, the more likely it is there'll be some prizewinners among them," May said, leading Carrie into the kitchen. On the kitchen table was a big bowl of fruit, a tall pitcher of iced tea, and two glasses. May invited Carrie to take a seat. Elise was listening to the radio and wiping down the counter; Carrie heard the tail end of a weather update on Hurricane Julius before Elise shut off the radio and walked out of the kitchen.

"Nasty business about that hurricane down south, isn't it?" May asked, pouring

Carrie some iced tea. "I remember when Hurricane Donna came up the Maine coast in 1960. Quite a mess. That was when hurricanes were named after women only," May added, shaking her head ruefully. "Then the women's movement got on the National Weather Service's case, and now they alternate between men's and women's names."

Carrie smiled as she reached for the tea. "Well, next year they can go from Hurricane Annie to Hurricane Billy to Hurricane Chloe," she joked as she poured herself a glass of tea. "Then they'll have to quit. Nothing could match Hurricane Chloe."

May smiled. "Believe me, my little Annie gives her a run for her money." She reached for the first of Carrie's boxes.

Carrie had arranged both boxes so that what she thought were her best photos were on top. May smiled as she flipped through a series of prints of the Civil War gun emplacements. Every so often May would put one of the prints aside, or mutter "magnificent" or "brilliant" under her breath.

Carrie sat there sipping her tea, trying to appear calm. But every time May uttered a compliment, her heart soared. *She really, really likes my work!* Carrie thought exultantly. *And this woman knows photographs.*

Carrie watched nervously as May came to the place in the second box where she'd arranged some of her photos of the poverty-ridden part of the island. There was not only the closeup of the outhouse with the broken door but also the shots of the dirty, hungry little girl and the sad-faced boy.

When May had gone through them all, the older woman looked closely at Carrie for several seconds without speaking. Carrie felt distinctly uncomfortable under her gaze.

"Are they okay?" Carrie asked finally.

May took a deep breath before she responded. Her gaze never left Carrie's face.

"Carrie Alden, I am choosing my words carefully because the last thing you need now, at this stage in your development as a photographer, is for someone to tell you how great you are," May said slowly. "Nonetheless," she continued, "these pictures are great."

Carrie's heart leaped again. *May Spencer-Rumsey, publisher of the most famous photo books on the planet, just said my pictures are great. Tell me I am not dreaming.*

May reached for an apple and shined it on a white cloth napkin. "Of course, I'll never be able to use several of the very best ones," she said matter-of-factly.

Carrie's jaw nearly bounced off her chest. "Wha . . . what do you mean?" she asked.

"Just that," May said, taking a bite of the apple.

"I'm sorry, May, I don't understand."

May carefully chewed the apple and took her time sipping her tea before she answered. "Because, my dear, some of these photographs are just plain wrong."

"Wrong?" Carrie repeated. "If the shots are good, how can they be wrong?"

"You have a lot to learn about the publishing business, dear," May replied, her tone turning brusque. "I'm running a for-profit publishing house here, not the *National Geographic*. This book we're doing is supposed to make money, not be an unprofitable exposé. To make money, we show what's beautiful, not what's ugly and depressing."

"But . . . but . . . but . . ." Carrie sounded like an outboard motor low on gas.

"Those pictures of the shacks are ugly and depressing. Not in my book!" May said firmly.

"But these people I met on the other side of the island—the ones who are part of an organization called COPE—said that all of this is the real Sunset Island. And I think they have a point!" Carrie cried.

"Ah, yes, COPE," May said. "I know all about them. Well, everybody has a cause. That is not my problem." She gave Carrie a piercing look. "Reality, my dear, can be whatever we choose to see."

"I . . . I just don't understand," Carrie stammered.

"Oh, I think you understand more than you give yourself credit for," May said coolly. "Look at other parts of America, for example. There's poverty, sexism, racism—all horrible things. But we don't think about them every day. In fact, most of us choose not to really see them at all. No, we see what we want to see, and that is what is real."

Tears welled up in Carrie's eyes, and she fought for self-control. "Isn't that all the more reason to show all sides of a place or an issue?" she said softly. She looked down at the little girl's face. It seemed to be pleading with her from the photograph. "This is just as real as the beach or the cliffs or a great blue heron in flight! If people on Sunset Island knew about this, they would want to make it better! We have an opportunity to show them!"

May gave Carrie a shrewd look. "Next you'll be telling me we have an *obligation* to show them."

"Well, we do!" Carrie blurted out.

May folded her hands and looked down for a moment. "Look, Carrie, I think you're a lovely and talented young girl. But you see everything as very black and white, and that's not the way the real world is."

"But—" Carrie began.

"No buts, Carrie," May said firmly. "There's nothing to discuss. No matter what the people from COPE think, it's just possible that those people from that slum have no one but themselves to blame for their problems. My family started out poor, too."

"Well, maybe someone gave your family a helping hand!" Carrie said heatedly. She couldn't believe she was arguing with May Spencer-Rumsey, and yet she couldn't seem to help herself. *You are ruining everything!* a voice screamed in her head.

"What I said upsets you?" May asked, her tone softer.

Carrie nodded, fighting back tears.

"You're young and this is your first book project," May said, somewhat condescendingly. "You'll soon learn that this is a business. If I'm putting your photos in a book, *I* decide which ones go in and which ones don't. It's called *editing.* If you don't think you can do this book my way, I'll find some other photographer who can," May said.

Carrie just sat there, trying to steady her trembling hands. She didn't know what to say or do.

Finally she stood and gathered up her photographs. "I . . . I guess I have to think about this," she said quietly.

"Fine, think about it," May said, nodding. "But call me tomorrow."

"Okay," Carrie said as May opened the front door for her. "But I honestly don't know what I'll tell you."

May smiled at her. "I hope you make the smart choice, Carrie," she said.

The smart choice? But what was smart and what was stupid? Carrie managed to hold back her tears while the uniformed young man got the car. Once she was alone, she cried all the way home.

When Carrie arrived at the Templetons', Josh, Becky, and Ian were waiting for her on the swing in front of the house. Carrie said hello, then excused herself and went inside. She called Emma, who agreed to meet Carrie at the Play Café that night at eight.

"I've just got to talk with you and Sam," Carrie said. "I am completely confused."

"About Billy and Josh?" Emma asked.

"No, about the photos for the book," Carrie said with a sigh. "I'll explain when I see you. It's too complicated to tell over the phone."

"Okay," Emma agreed. "I'll call Sam. I know she's got the night off."

"Thanks. Come prepared to give me some advice," Carrie warned her friend before hanging up.

"Becky's already in the car," Ian said, coming up to Carrie as she stepped onto the porch.

Right, Carrie reminded herself, *the big shopping date. I just about forgot.*

"Ready for our double date?" Josh asked with a grin, putting his arm around Ian's shoulder.

"Becky says it isn't really a date," Ian replied. "She says she'd die if anyone knew she went out with someone thirteen."

"Well, *we* know it's a date," Carrie said conspiratorially, "no matter what she calls it."

"Yeah," Ian agreed, a grin and a blush hitting his face simultaneously.

"Can we get going?" Becky called from the back seat as the others strolled slowly to the car. "Ian here is desperate for some new threads, especially since his gig is tomorrow night."

Becky kept suggesting different outfits to Ian the entire ride downtown. "Hmmm," she said, eyeing Ian critically in the back seat. "Lord Whitehead and the Zit Men. Maybe we could dress you in an English-royalty theme."

"I don't think so," Ian replied, trying to move closer to Becky without being obvious. "Not industrial enough."

"I've got it!" Becky shouted. Carrie turned her head slightly so she could hear Becky better. "You want industrial, right? How about if you guys all wear steel-worker's clothes? Blue-collar chic!"

Ian took her seriously. "I don't think so. But you might be on the right track."

"I'll drop you two right here," Carrie said, pulling the car to the curb outside Cheap Charlie's. "Josh and I will be back in an hour to pick you up."

"Okay," Becky said, jumping out of the

back seat. "Don't do anything I wouldn't do!" she added with a smirk.

Carrie rolled her eyes. "See you guys," she said as she pulled out into traffic.

"Where do you want to go?" Josh asked a few minutes later. Suddenly Carrie realized she was driving aimlessly.

"Let's drive out toward the dunes," she said. "I want to talk to you about what happened at May's house."

The drive out to the dunes was silent. Carrie stopped the car, got out, walked to the top of one of the big sand dunes overlooking the ocean, and sat down. Josh followed and sat behind her.

"So?" Josh asked. "Tell me about it."

Carrie gave Josh an abbreviated version of the events at Winterhaven, leaving out the part about how she had left in tears.

"So my problem is," she said, fidgeting with some seashells, "as much as I want my photos in the book, I'd feel like a traitor to the island if I didn't include those shots of the poor area and its residents. But if I tell her I want control over the book, she'll simply use a different photographer."

"Maybe she's just playing chicken with you," Josh reasoned as he kicked at the sand. "Maybe if you don't allow yourself to be dictated to, she'll have to use the photos you want."

"I don't think so," Carrie said with a sigh. "I think she's being completely straight with me. It's not like there aren't other photographers around. There are lots, and most would kill for this assignment," she added bitterly.

They got up and walked hand in hand for a while, Carrie lost in thought. *That's one great thing about being with Josh*, Carrie reflected fondly, looking at his profile. *It's perfectly okay for me not to say anything*.

When they got back to the car, Carrie kissed Josh lightly.

"What was that for?" he asked her, clearly pleased.

"For being you," Carrie said.

Carrie was preoccupied at dinner, even though Ian, who was dressed in his new performance outfit, did his best to get her attention. She was glad to leave to go to the Play Café to meet Sam and Emma, and glad that Josh was being understanding about it.

"Maybe we can go for a late drive later," he suggested in the driveway.

"Maybe," Carrie agreed, getting in the car.

Josh stuck his head in the window and smiled down at Carrie. "Don't worry so much, Car," he said easily. "I know you'll do the right thing."

Carrie smiled back at him. But as she drove away she realized she had no idea what the right thing was. Not about her photography, and not about Billy and Josh.

Carrie was completely preoccupied when she arrived at the Play Café. She saw Emma and Sam sitting at their usual table, and bravely greeted them as she sat down. They'd already ordered a diet soda for her.

"Hey, girlfriend," Sam teased, "lighten up! You are nineteen, cute, and single! What could be bad? Are you pregnant?"

Carrie shook her head.

"Then what's got you so down?" Emma chimed in. "I've never seen you this way before."

Carrie took a big swallow of soda before answering. Then she proceeded to give Sam and Emma an hour-by-hour account of the last couple of days—her photography trip with Kurt, the poverty-stricken community, meeting Jade and learning about COPE, seeing Billy with Diana De Witt the night before, and her bad meeting with May Spencer-Rumsey that afternoon. As she talked she unconsciously scribbled spirals on a paper napkin.

"Wow," Sam said half seriously when Carrie was finished. "I take it back. You really do have problems!"

"Yeah," Carrie agreed glumly.

"But not insurmountable problems," Emma assured her. "Which do you want to talk about first?"

"The photography book," Carrie replied. "My guy problems are an ongoing dilemma."

"That's my girl!" Sam agreed. "Too many men is a problem that can wait."

Carrie ignored Sam and tried to explain her problem. "The thing is, if I let May edit my photographs for her book, then people won't get an honest view of Sunset Island."

"So?" Sam asked.

"So there's a lot of beauty here, but there's a whole other side to the island that no one wants to see!" Carrie explained.

Emma nodded. "I didn't even know about it. Kurt never took me there," she added, sounding a bit hurt.

"Don't be offended, Emma," Carrie said. "He only showed me because he thought there was a chance of getting that information out in this book."

"Not if this woman has her way," Emma

pointed out. "I don't think it's right for her to choose your pictures. That's sort of like censorship."

Sam made a face.

"What are you doing that for?" Carrie asked her.

"Because this is just so ridiculous!" Sam said. "It's easy for you to say it's censorship, Em. You don't have to work for a living."

"You always say that whenever I have an opinion that differs from yours," Emma shot at Sam.

"But I'm right!" Sam countered. "You don't know what it's like! It's not your fault or anything; it's just the way it is!"

"Well, thank you so much," Emma said frostily.

"Don't go into your Kat voice just because you're ticked at me," Sam said. She was referring to Emma's mother, Katerina Cresswell, who had perfected a miffed tone that could freeze a fire.

"Sorry," Emma apologized. Carrie knew Emma couldn't stand sounding like her mother, whom she loathed. "I just don't believe in censorship of art, and I'd feel the same way if I were poor."

Sam dribbled Coke from her straw back into her glass and cocked her head thoughtfully. "The way I see it, Carrie, you're getting paid to do this book. It's a job. Your boss is this publisher. If she wants to publish only pictures of dead fish, I suggest you let her publish pictures of dead fish. Take the money and run, babe."

"But I owe it to the people of this island to tell an honest story!" Carrie cried. "I know I didn't know about all of this before, but it's been there all along. I can't just pretend it doesn't exist."

"That's right!" Emma agreed.

"Please," Sam said disdainfully. "She's not asking you to rob a bank. Just do the stupid book. Look at all the doors it will open for you!"

"I don't know, Sam. I just don't know," Carrie said softly. Her eye caught the large clock on the wall. She was surprised that so much time had passed, and absolutely nothing was settled in her mind. "I better go," she sighed, getting up. "Josh is waiting for me."

"We didn't even get to the guy stuff!" Sam protested.

"Guess not," Carrie agreed. She headed home from the Play Café, May Spencer-Rumsey's words echoing in her mind. *I hope you make the smart choice*, she had said.

"But what does that mean?" Carrie yelled with frustration, pounding her hand on the steering wheel. Unfortunately, there was no clear answer, not even from her own heart.

EIGHT

Carrie woke up and stared out the window at the cloudy sky. It looked as pensive as she felt. She'd tossed and turned the night before, trying to figure out what to tell May Spencer-Rumsey.

What if she *did* do the book, and then donated any profits she made to COPE? Wouldn't that make the most sense of all? On the other hand, she had all those expenses from school. She really could use the money.

The phone rang in the hall, and Carrie sprang out of bed to answer it.

"Templeton residence," she said into the mouthpiece.

"Carrie, dear, it's May. Hope I didn't wake you."

"Oh, no, I was up," Carrie assured her.

"Unlike most people in publishing, I'm an early riser," May said jovially. "Let me get to the reason of my call. I know that when you left here yesterday, you felt unsure about your involvement in the project."

"Yes," Carrie admitted.

"I hope this doesn't sound condescending," May said carefully, "but you really are very young. Very young and, as I told you yesterday, very talented."

"Thank you," Carrie said quietly.

"Yes, well, it's your youth and inexperience that are getting in the way here, dear," May explained.

"It just seems to me that COPE has some very strong points," Carrie said softly.

"That may be so," May agreed. "But Carrie, there are a million causes in this world. I give more than my fair share to charity. I can't get involved with every organization that bangs on my door, now, can I?"

"I guess not," Carrie said faintly.

"But let me get to exactly why I called you," May said briskly. "I'm having a private show at the Sunset Gallery tomorrow. On exhibit will be some of my favorite photos of Sunset Island. I'd like to include your work in the exhibit."

An exhibit at the Sunset Gallery? Carrie thought she'd die from excitement. "That's fabulous!" she cried.

"I thought you might feel that way," May said with a chuckle. "And since I recall you admiring my David Frohman photograph so much, I thought you'd be interested to know that he'll be my house guest that evening, and he'll be attending the exhibit."

"You mean I'll actually get to meet David Frohman?" Carrie squeaked.

"You'll actually get David Frohman to see your work," May corrected Carrie with a laugh. "I take it this means yes."

"Yes!" Carrie agreed happily.

"You understand that if I'm to promote your work, we can't have any more silliness about my choices for the book, all right?" May asked.

"All right," Carrie agreed. The words just popped out of her mouth.

"Fine, then," May said. "I'm glad we've worked this out. I'll choose some of my favorites from the shots you left here, and I'll see you there at six o'clock."

"May I bring a guest?" Carrie asked May. She was thinking how thrilled Josh would be to meet David Frohman.

"My dear, you are part of the show, which gives you a certain amount of clout." May laughed. "Call the gallery and put whomever you like on the guest list."

"Thank you so much!" Carrie replied.

"My pleasure," May said, and hung up.

Carrie threw on her robe and rushed downstairs to see if Josh was up. She had to tell him the news. She found him out by the pool, reading the morning paper.

"So isn't that incredible?" Carrie cried when she'd finished telling him about her phone conversation.

"The gallery show is great, and you know I'd love to meet David Frohman," Josh said slowly, "but what happened to all those misgivings you had yesterday about her editing your work for the book?"

"I know," Carrie admitted, pensively re-tying the sash on her robe.

"So, when did you decide to abide by her wishes?" Josh asked quietly. "Was it when she offered you the chance to be part of the gallery show?"

Carrie stood up and stared into the pool, then looked back at Josh. "Is it really so terrible?" she asked him plaintively. "May says the book is supposed to be a beautiful photographic essay about the island, not an exposé."

"I guess you could look at it that way," Josh agreed.

But Carrie knew him too well. He didn't

have to tell her he thought she was wrong. Well, *she* didn't think she was wrong! And it was her decision!

Carrie looked at Josh another few moments, then turned and ran upstairs to shower and dress. She knew that Chloe would be up any minute. Claudia and Graham almost always slept late, but the children didn't.

I'm tired of worrying about what Josh thinks, what Billy thinks, what my friends think, Carrie thought, scrubbing shampoo into her scalp. *I can make my own decisions!*

When she came back downstairs Josh was feeding Ian and Chloe his famous cheesy eggs, and Carrie's mood softened. Josh was such a great guy. He was only telling her what he thought was right.

"Want some eggs?" Josh asked as he slipped some toast onto Chloe's plate.

"Thanks," Carrie said, smiling at him. She kissed him lightly on the lips. "And that's your official good morning."

"Dog germs!" Chloe screamed.

Everyone cracked up. "What do you mean, 'dog germs'?" Carrie asked her.

"When Snoopy kisses Lucy in the comics,

she yells, 'dog germs!'" Chloe explained patiently. "Daddy reads *Peanuts* to me."

"Well, she says that because Snoopy is a dog," Carrie said, getting the milk out of the refrigerator.

Chloe munched on a bite of toast. "I thought she said that because kisses gave you dog germs," she said.

"Only if you kiss an ugly girl." Ian guffawed.

Carrie and Josh stared at him.

"Get it? Ugly girl? Dog?" Ian asked.

"Sorry, buddy, not funny," Josh said, pouring himself a cup of coffee.

"I bet Becky would think it was funny," he mumbled into his plate.

"Becky is not someone I would consider an arbiter of good taste," Carrie said mildly.

"Let's watch music videos," Chloe said. She had recently found out that Annie loved to watch music videos, so now she did, too. "Can I take my plate into the family room?" she asked Carrie.

"Okay," Carrie said. She wasn't in the mood to argue.

"I gotta watch, too," Ian said, following her. "I gotta see if there are any cool moves I should use in my gig tonight."

Carrie went in, too, turned on the TV, and

finished her breakfast. She watched Ian as he avidly watched the videos, occasionally moving an arm or leg in imitation of what he saw on the screen.

Carrie sent up a silent prayer. *Please don't let him be as awful as I think he's going to be.*

"And now a National Weather Service advisory on Hurricane Julius," the announcer on the music video station said. "Hurricane warnings have been lifted for the coastlines of Georgia, South Carolina, and North Carolina, as the storm veered still farther north this afternoon. A hurricane watch has been posted for the area from Virginia Beach, Virginia, north to New York City. Julius now sports maximum winds of one hundred and five miles per hour. The next advisory will be in two hours."

"What's a hurricane?" Chloe asked, finishing the last of her toast.

"A big storm," Carrie answered.

"Worse than a storm," Ian scoffed. "It's a mega-storm with really high winds that can lift a house right into the air and send it crashing back down in a million, trillion pieces."

Chloe's eyes grew wide. "A doll's house?"

"No, stupid, a person's house," Ian said.

"Don't call her stupid," Carrie said with a frown. This was not like Ian at all. He was usually sweet to Chloe.

"Sheesh," Ian muttered, and stomped out of the room.

"He's nervous about tonight," Josh explained.

Chloe's eyes were filling with tears. "What if that hurricane comes here and smashes our house?"

Carrie sat next to Chloe and put her arm around the little girl. "It's not coming here," Carrie assured her. "It's very, very far away."

"But what if it did?" Chloe persisted.

"Well, then, your mommy and your daddy would make sure that you got far away and were very safe," Carrie promised.

A new rap group started doing an up-tempo tune, and soon Chloe was distracted by the dancing. Carrie and Josh carried the dirty breakfast plates into the kitchen.

"Kids' minds amaze me," Josh said as he helped Carrie load the dishwasher.

"Yeah," Carrie said absently. The vision of the little boy playing on the porch right near the fetid swamp popped into her head. What would happen to him if a hurricane hit the island? Who would protect *him?*

"You're sure this looks okay? Swear to God?" Ian asked Carrie as he ran his hand through his newly slicked-back hair. Ian was dressed for his gig at the Play Café in the clothes that Becky had picked out for him. He had on a black T-shirt under a studded black leather vest, black jeans, and black cowboy boots. All the black made him look even smaller than he was. And the slicked-back hair gave him a sort of junior-Mafia look.

"Well, the cowboy boots certainly make you taller," Carrie managed. She was not about to say anything to undermine Ian's already shaky confidence.

"You look like you just stepped out of a gangster movie," Graham told his son when he walked into the family room.

Ian's face fell. "I look like dog meat."

"No, you don't," Claudia assured him, shooting her husband a nasty look. "Black is very hot-looking on stage."

Ian didn't look convinced, but just then a car honked in the driveway. "That's Donald," Ian said, naming the boy in his band who played the microwave. "Well, I gotta go now so we can do a sound check," he told the group. "I'll see you there."

"Don't you dare do or say anything to make him feel bad," Claudia warned her husband after Ian had left. "This is a very big night for him."

"Yes, Claudia," Graham said with a grin, kissing his wife on the back of the neck.

"I mean it, Graham," she said, turning around to face him.

Graham held his hands up in the air. "Hey, I got him this gig, didn't I?"

"And that's another thing," Claudia said. "Don't ever tell him that's how he got it. He'd be mortified."

"My lips are sealed," Graham said solemnly.

Claudia put her arms around her husband's neck. "Being your son isn't always easy for him, you know," she said softly. She kissed him lightly.

"Dog germs!" Chloe screeched, running into the room.

"Dog germs!" Graham screeched back at the little girl, then chased her around the room while she screamed with laughter.

An hour later, Claudia, Graham, Chloe, Carrie, and Josh had piled into the Templetons' new van and headed over to the Play

Café. It was already very crowded with all the younger kids on the island.

As the group made their way into the club, people had very visible reactions to seeing Graham Templeton. Some got quiet, some yelled, and some bold ones thrust things in his face to get his autograph.

"This is exactly why we don't go out to clubs much," Claudia leaned over to whisper to Carrie.

Josh led the way to the table up front that was reserved for them.

"Well, hello, young lady," came a voice behind Carrie as soon as she sat down. Carrie turned around. It was Jade Meader. She was sitting at the next table with a pretty young girl.

"Hi, Jade," Carrie said, genuinely glad to see the older woman. "I didn't know you were a rock fan."

"She loves it," the young girl said with a laugh. "Elton John and you-know-who are her favorites." It was visible that the you-know-who the girl meant was Graham, seated on the other side of the table.

"Well, then, let me introduce you," Carrie said, and introduced Graham and Claudia to Jade and the young girl.

"It's a true pleasure," Jade said. "'Do

What's Right'" is one of my all-time favorite songs," she added, naming one of Graham's biggest hits, which was about helping the homeless.

"Gram loves causes," the girl said, rolling her eyes.

"Yes I do," Jade said, giving her granddaughter an affectionate look. "This is Tisha," she said, "my eldest grandchild. She doesn't approve of causes."

Carrie attempted to smile, but she felt terribly guilty. Her decision about the photography book had suddenly leaped into her mind. Was she doing what was right? She had a feeling Jade wouldn't think so.

"I'm glad I ran into you, Carrie," Jade continued. "I thought you might be interested in an event that COPE is planning."

"I would!" Carrie said eagerly. *Maybe if I do volunteer work for COPE, I won't feel so guilty about the book*, she thought.

"Great," Jade said. "We're meeting at Rubie's tomorrow evening, and then we plan to go over to the Sunset Gallery to picket their photo exhibit."

"Their photo exhibit?" Carrie echoed dully.

Jade nodded. "There's a wealthy well-known publisher on the island by the name of May Spencer-Rumsey," she continued. "She's having a private show tomorrow of photographs of the island. We've tried everything we can think of to get her attention—let's hope this will do it!"

"But . . . but why would you picket her?" Carrie asked in a quavering voice.

"Because she's only going to show photographs of the beautiful people and their beautiful lives, I guarantee it," Jade said firmly. "We've got a COPE member who works part-time at the gallery. She told me about all the shots that are being hung."

"Did she?" Carrie asked dully.

"She did," Jade confirmed. "This could be our opportunity to really get people on the island to stand up and take notice of us, instead of sweeping these issues under the rug."

Oh my God, Carrie thought, *I can't tell her my photographs are there. I just can't.*

NINE

"I . . . I'm busy tomorrow night," Carrie said lamely.

"Too bad," Jade said. "Well, another time, then."

"Sure," Carrie answered, attempting a smile. She could feel Josh's eyes on her from behind.

Fortunately she was saved from having to make further conversation by the owner of the Play Café, who stood up at the microphone.

"Thanks for coming, everyone. Before we get started, you should know that we've just had a hurricane warning posted for Hurricane Julius."

A murmur went up in the crowd.

"There's still a real good chance the hurricane will miss us completely, but they've just issued Sunset Island a warning for the next forty-eight hours. And now, ready to make their own musical hurricane, is a group I haven't had the pleasure of hearing yet, but I'm sure they're terrific. Please welcome Lord Whitehead and the Zit Men!"

Everyone applauded as Ian and his friends bounded onto the stage. Carrie could see Becky and Allie right down in front. Becky waved wildly at Ian, who smiled and blushed in response.

"Thank you very much," Ian said into the mike. "This first tune is a classic, done the Zit Men way." He lifted his sticks and stood over his washing machine. "One, two, one-two-three-four!"

Ian pressed the play button on his cassette player, and the sounds of Lou Reed singing "Gloria" filled the room. But before the recording had gone for ten seconds, the Zit Men joined in on their "instruments"—microwave, toaster oven, etc.

When the chorus came, the Zit Men screamed along with Lou Reed. "*G-L-O-R-I-A*, Gloooo-ri-a!" and beat even harder on their household appliances.

"That's the most awful thing I ever heard!" Tisha told her grandmother.

"Maybe they're making a political statement," Jade yelled back.

Graham put his head in his hands. Everyone was turning around to look at him. They all knew Ian was his son.

"You have two seconds to put a look of total pride on your face," Claudia hissed at her husband.

Graham lifted his head and tried to smile in the direction of the stage.

"*G-L-O-R-I-A*, Glooor-i-a!" the Zit Men howled, then banged some more in a painful assault on the ears.

"Boooooooo!" someone yelled in the crowd. "You suck!"

The song finished to complete silence. Then Graham put his hands together and started clapping. Slowly other people joined in, until finally there was a tepid round of applause.

Somehow Ian and his band made it through four songs before mercifully being replaced by the next band. Ian ran off the stage. He looked like he was going to cry.

"I'll go talk to him," Graham said, pushing himself out of his chair.

"No, I will," Carrie said quickly. "That is, if you don't mind," she added. "It's just that I have a feeling he'd be completely humiliated to see you right now."

"Carrie's right," Claudia said softly.

Carrie headed across the room.

"Hey, Carrie!" Becky cried when she saw her. "That was the worst excuse for music I have ever heard in my life!"

"Well, he's new at it," Carrie said gently. She tried to move past the girl.

But Becky grabbed her arm. "All Ian had to do was to listen to me! I told him he'd be a big success if he'd just cover his dad's tunes!" Becky cried. "Why didn't he just listen to me?"

"You'll have to ask him," Carrie said, trying to escape Becky's clutches.

"Listen," Becky continued, "everyone knows I went shopping with him yesterday. Everyone knows we've been hanging out. I am, like, totally humiliated!"

"Well, that's your problem," Carrie said, and walked away. At the moment she had no time for Becky's endless self-involvement.

"Yeah, but—" Becky protested from somewhere behind her. Carrie ignored her and made her way through the crowd to the area behind the stage, where there was a small dressing room for the musicians.

Carrie found Ian by himself in the corner, his head down on his folded arms. The rest of the Zit Men were nowhere to be seen.

"Hi," Carrie said softly, sitting down next to Ian.

"Go away," Ian mumbled through his hands. His voice sounded as if he'd been crying.

Carrie just sat there next to him for a while, listening to the next band. When the song finished, Carrie could hear the crowd clapping and hooting.

"They love that band," Ian said miserably. "I should just kill myself."

"From what I've heard, all that band can do is covers of Aerosmith," Carrie said, choosing her words carefully. "They try to sound exactly like them."

"So?" Ian asked from behind his arms.

"So you tried to do something different," Carrie said. "That's very risky, but it's also very brave."

"Brave?" Ian asked, lifting up his sorrowful face. "How about stupid? How about idiotic? How about I can never show my face on this island again?"

"Okay, don't," Carrie said simply.

"Yeah, right." Ian snorted. "What am I supposed to do, run away?"

"If you want," Carrie said.

"Everyone thinks I'm a big nothing," Ian said, gulping hard. "Even Dad." He thought

141

about this a moment. "*Especially* Dad," he added bitterly.

Carrie stood up and wandered around the tiny dressing room. "Let me ask you a question," she finally said. "Do you think that when your dad got started in music, he was instantly a big success?"

"I know he wasn't," Ian said. "He sang for tips at this bar on the Jersey shore. He said everyone was drunk, and no one listened unless he covered a Bruce Springsteen tune or something."

"So they wouldn't listen to him because he was trying to do something original," Carrie said slowly.

Ian stared at Carrie and made a face. "I know what you're getting at, but this is different."

"How?" she asked, coming back to sit by Ian. "You went out there and did something original. Okay, it wasn't a total success," she acknowledged. "That doesn't mean you should just give up!"

Ian picked up one of his sticks from the table in front of him. "People thought rap sucked at first," he said to himself.

"Right!" Carrie encouraged him.

"Maybe they're just not used to industrial

music—it's pretty radical stuff," he added seriously.

"The thing is, when it comes to art, you have to decide what's right for *you*," Carrie said earnestly. "If you believe in it and keep working at it, then no matter what happens, you're not a failure. But if you just give up, or give in to what someone else thinks you should be, then you're not a real artist at all."

And as these words were leaving Carrie's mouth she wondered, *Am I talking to Ian, or am I really talking to myself?*

The Templetons, Josh, and Carrie rode home in silence. Ian went straight up to his room and shut the door.

"What did you say to him backstage?" Josh asked Carrie.

"I tried to tell him that the real failure is in not trying, or in giving up just because he came up against an obstacle, things like that," Carrie said, plopping down on the family room couch.

"Did it help?" Josh asked, sitting next to her.

"Honestly, I have no idea," Carrie admitted. "I sounded like my own mother, if you

143

want to know the truth," she added with a sigh.

"Hey, your mother's a very classy lady!" Josh said with a smile.

"I know that," Carrie agreed. "I just meant I sounded *old*."

"I'm going to take Chloe upstairs and give her a bath," Claudia said, coming into the family room.

"Want me to do it?" Carrie asked quickly. She was feeling guilty about not working hard enough—not only had she taken a lot of time off recently because of her photography, but Josh was there, too.

"No, it's cool," Claudia said. "But you could make a salad for dinner in about an hour, and heat up that chili, okay?"

"Sure," Carrie answered. After Claudia left the room, she turned to Josh. "Listen, I'm going to run upstairs and call Emma and Sam. They still don't know about the gallery show tomorrow night and I want to invite them."

"Speaking of the show," Josh said, "what are you going to do about COPE? I heard everything that woman said to you, you know."

She stood up. "I have a right to have my

photos in a show," she said. She sounded defensive and she knew it.

"And I guess they have a right to picket," Josh answered reasonably.

"It's a free country," Carrie said stiffly.

"Yeah," Josh agreed, "but it's not an *equal* country. I think that's her whole point."

To that, Carrie had absolutely no response.

Carrie ran upstairs, dialed Sam's number, stretched the extension cord so she could pull the hall phone into her room, and sat on her bed.

"Jacobs residence," came Sam's voice through the phone.

"Hi, it's me," Carrie said.

"Hi there!" Sam said. "Hey, what happened at Ian's gig, anyway? Becky and Allie's friend just dropped them off, and Becky came in screaming that Ian had, and I quote, 'like totally humiliated her with his dorkiness,' end quote."

"She didn't think Ian's band was very good," Carrie said.

"Is she right?" Sam asked.

"Yes," Carrie confessed. "But imagine how he feels! That girl is so self-involved, Sam!"

"Well, you know Becky," Sam said. "Every sentence in her vocabulary begins with the letter *I*."

"Listen, I wanted to tell you—" Carrie began.

"Hold on a second, Carrie," Sam said. "Allie, don't eat the fudge right before dinner! I just stuck the chicken in the oven!"

"This is one of my fat days, and I want fudge!" Carrie heard Allie yell.

"Sorry, Carrie," Sam said into the phone. "You were saying?"

"I made a decision about the book. I decided to do it."

"Smart girl!" Sam cheered.

"Thanks," Carrie said. She had known that would be Sam's reaction. That was exactly why she'd called Sam instead of Emma. "And listen to this," she continued. "Tomorrow night some of my photos will be exhibited in this ritzy private show at the Sunset Gallery. May set it all up."

"Wow, that is so cool!" Sam cried. "I am so psyched for you!"

"Thanks," Carrie said gratefully. It felt wonderful to have someone completely approve of her decision.

"So, I wanted to invite you," she continued. "Emma, too, unless she disapproves so

146

much she won't want to come," Carrie added ruefully.

"Hey, Emma's not like that," Sam said loyally. "She can't help it if she was born with a silver spoon in her mouth. I mean, she has no idea what life is like for real people, know what I mean?"

"I do," Carrie agreed.

"Anyway, of course I'll be there, and I'm sure Emma will come, too," Sam said. "Hey, I bet tons of rich guys come to private art shows. What do you think?"

"I think you should come in one of your to-die-for outfits and watch them grovel at your feet," Carrie answered with a laugh.

"Good plan," Sam commented. "Want me to call Emma for you?"

"Would you?" Carrie asked. "I don't know, I feel sort of . . ."

"Funny," Sam filled in for her. "Well, I don't. Hey, the three of us can't always agree. It's not such a big deal!"

Carrie gave Sam all the details about when the show began before hanging up. She only hoped that Emma would be as happy for her as Sam was. And that COPE wouldn't really picket a show that could change her life.

TEN

Carrie sat down on her bed. She had just caught herself biting her nails for the fifteenth time that day. *Come on,* she said to herself, *you're about to have the first major photo show of your life at age nineteen. You should be celebrating, not chewing on your fingers like a child.* And then another voice inside her head said, *Yeah, but most people don't get their first show picketed!*

It was four-thirty in the afternoon, and Carrie was due at the Sunset Gallery in an hour. *I'd better get dressed,* she thought. The show, May Spencer-Rumsey had reminded her by phone early that afternoon, started at six. *As if I need reminding!* Carrie thought ruefully.

"You might want to arrive a half-hour early," May had said, "to give yourself a chance to meet some of the other photogra-

phers who are being exhibited. David
Frohman, in particular, has expressed an
interest in talking with you."

Carrie's heart, which had been pounding
ever since she awoke that morning, had
gone into overdrive.

"David Frohman wants to talk with *me?*"
Carrie had asked incredulously. "I'm just a
kid!"

"My dear, you are the youngest photographer who has ever been granted an exhibit
at the Sunset Gallery," May had responded.
"I imagine quite a number of people will
want to talk with you. Perhaps even the
Boston *Globe.*"

"What are you talking about?" Carrie had
asked. *The Boston* Globe? *That's the biggest
newspaper in New England. Why would
they be at this show? Good grief—they're
going to review it.*

"You *are* young!" May had laughed. "You
forget that I have a fair amount of pull with
the press. The *Globe* said they might send a
reviewer. Depends on what happens with
that nasty storm to the south. Anyway, I
must run. See you there!"

"May?"

"Yes, Carrie?"

Carrie had been embarrassed to ask the

next question, but swallowed her pride. "Uh . . . what should I wear?" she had said sheepishly. *Well, she can't expect me to know everything.*

May had laughed again. "My dear, you're the artist! People expect you to be original. Wear whatever you want. See you at five-thirty!" And she had hung up.

Be original, Carrie repeated to herself as she stood in front of her closet. Absolutely nothing in her closet looked at all original to her. Finally she pulled out a flowing flowered skirt in green and white and a white leotard. With this outfit she wore little white ballet slippers. She brushed her hair until the golden highlights sparkled in her thick chestnut hair, and surveyed herself in the mirror. *Oh, what the hell* Carrie thought to herself, and added some lipstick. This was a big deal—Carrie never wore makeup.

When she went downstairs to meet Josh, who was waiting for her in the Templetons' living room, he gave a mock wolf whistle of appreciation.

"Hey, you look outrageously great!" he said, making his eyes comically big. "What say you and I skip this shindig and adjourn back to your dressing area?" he joked, af-

fecting the greasy tone of a sleazy Holly-
wood executive.

Carrie twirled around the room, enjoying
Josh's attention. "Sorry," she joked back,
"art before love. Let's hit the road, buster."

They left for the gallery. Carrie was truly
excited. *Please, God*, she thought as they
sped down the street, *just don't let there be
any demonstration.*

So far, so good, Carrie said to herself,
looking out the gallery window at five-forty-
five. *Lots of people waiting to come in, and
no demonstrators.*

Emma and Sam had been waiting for her
at the gallery when she and Josh arrived, as
Carrie had put their names on the special
guest list that okayed them for early admis-
sion to the show. That let Carrie know that
Sam was really excited—she *never* arrived
anywhere early!

"Hi," Carrie said shyly to Emma.

"I'm so proud of you," Emma said, giving
her a hug.

"I thought you might be . . . I don't
know . . . mad," Carrie said with a shrug.

"Never!" Emma protested. "This is a
great night for you, and that's that," she
added firmly.

"Hey, Car, you look great," Sam said, giving Carrie a hug. "You do fill out a leotard, girl."

Carrie laughed and Josh put his arm around her. "Sam speaks the truth," he said. "Bodacious, smart, and talented—what a girl!"

"Here, here!" Sam cried.

"You guys . . ." Carrie said, shaking her head. But really, she couldn't have felt any happier. *I have the world's greatest friends,* she thought. *And wow, do Emma and Sam look sensational!*

Emma had chosen a typical Emma Cresswell outfit—absolutely right for the occasion and not a thread out of place. She had on a tightly pleated white silk skirt with a matching sleeveless silk blouse, and a white bejeweled barrette was in her hair. Sam, as usual, had dressed more outrageously in a tight red miniskirt and a black suede mock turtleneck. The top looked perfectly ordinary from the front, but when she spun around for Carrie's benefit Carrie saw that it had a big diamond cut out of the back making it obvious that she wore no bra. As usual, she had on her trademark red cowboy boots, but she'd added a rhinestone ankle bracelet around the left boot. That was Sam!

"Shall we?" Josh asked with mock formality, giving Carrie his arm.

"We shall," Carrie answered gaily.

The foursome headed for the far corner of the gallery, where eight of Carrie's photographs were hung. Carrie herself had supervised the hanging that morning.

"Your photos are awesome!" Sam exclaimed. "Look at this one!" she said, pointing to an eight-by-ten of lobster pots stacked in crazy-quilt fashion on a tidy dock.

"I like that one a lot," Carrie admitted.

"Carrie Alden!" a familiar voice called from behind her.

May Spencer-Rumsey stood near the door.

A muscular, ruggedly handsome man with a twinkle in his intelligent eyes stood with her. *David Frohman. I'd recognize him anywhere.*

"Come here, Carrie," May continued. "I'd like you to meet someone before they let the mob in. There's not much time."

Carrie excused herself from her friends and walked slowly across the gallery. She felt like a million eyes were on her, but actually only May and David Frohman were watching her.

"Carrie," May said, "I'd like to introduce you to David Frohman. David, Carrie Alden, one of the finest young photographers in America, even if America doesn't know it yet." May, as usual, knew the right thing to say at the right moment.

David reached out a callused hand, and Carrie shook it.

"It's an honor to meet you, sir."

"Please, call me David!" he said with a laugh. "You make me feel ancient!"

"David," Carrie said shyly. "You've been my idol ever since I saw that famous shot you took for *Life* magazine." Carrie was referring to a Pulitzer Prize–winning photo of an elderly couple sitting on a park bench in front of a mural that had zebras painted on it. The couple looked like they were about to be devoured by the zebras, and yet their expressions were normal, even banal. The photo's juxtaposition of the exotic and the ordinary had been lauded all across America.

"Right place, right time." Frohman shrugged modestly. "For every one like that, there are a thousand that aren't right."

Carrie nodded. *I'll remember that*, she thought.

"I feel the same way about my wife," Frohman continued.

"That I'm one of the thousand that aren't right?" came a pleasant voice from behind David.

He turned around and put his arm around an elegant woman with short blond hair. "Hey, I meant that the other thousand couldn't fill your shoes!" he protested.

"Just checking," she said with a twinkle in her eye. She put her arm around her husband's waist.

"Edine," David said, "I'd like you to meet Carrie Alden. Carrie, my wife, Edine."

"Nice to meet you, Carrie," Edine said with a smile.

"Carrie took the picture of the blue heron over there." Frohman pointed meaningfully to the far corner.

"Did you?" Edine asked. "It's excellent! I think you have wonderful compositional skills," she added with a smile.

"I suggest we move away from the door, gang," Frohman interrupted as the gallery staff moved to let in the crowd that had gathered outside. "It's showtime!" he added, raising his eyebrows comically.

A huge crowd of people—it looked to

Carrie like a hundred or more—entered the Sunset Gallery all at once. Some of them headed directly to the photos that were hung on the walls and on temporary white partitions. But Carrie saw that a good portion of the people went straight to the long tables of wine and cheese that were along one of the walls.

Look at those clothes! Carrie thought, checking out the expensive outfits that most of the gallery-goers were wearing. *These people are all incredibly well-dressed. And rich. And noisy!* Carrie frowned at the din coming from the people sipping wine and gobbling down cheese. Many of them hadn't even looked at the photos at all! She noticed David Frohman looking at her.

"Like I said," Frohman observed, winking conspiratorially at her, "it's showtime."

"These people are here as much to look at each other as to look at our photos!" Carrie exclaimed, surveying the crowd.

"Bingo!" Frohman said. "You're young, but you're learning."

All of a sudden, a few groups of people started moving toward the front window of the gallery—the window facing Main Street—and pointing out. Carrie went to look. Her heart sank at what she saw.

Outside, a group of about ten people of all ages were readying picket signs. Jade was there, and she carried a megaphone.

Oh, no, this can't really be happening! Carrie thought frantically. She looked on as the group formed a picket line and started walking back and forth on the sidewalk in front of the gallery. Show the Real Island! one sign read. It's Our Island, Too! read another. The crowd chanted, "Hey, hey, what do you say? Summer people ought to pay!" referring to the fact that COPE wanted summer visitors to pay higher taxes so the less wealthy year-round residents could improve their sewer system, among other things.

"Well, I see Jade is as good as her word," Josh said, coming up beside Carrie.

Carrie felt sick to her stomach. She fled to the back of the gallery, where Emma and Sam were chatting. Josh trailed behind her. Shaken, she told them that the people from COPE had started to picket the show.

"COPE? But I thought they were your friends!" Sam exclaimed.

"They don't know my photos are in the show," Carrie explained. "Not that I think it would make any difference."

"Is Kurt out there with them?" Emma asked, her eyes wide.

"I didn't see him," Carrie said.

"Well, so what if they're picketing?" Sam asked. "They've got a right to picket. And you have a right to have your photos shown in here. Anyway, they don't seem to be making much of an impression." Sam motioned to the packed gallery. People were chatting and looking at the photos. No one was paying the demonstrators any mind at all.

Emma sighed. "Do you think Jade's going to be mad at you for exhibiting your photos here?" she asked Carrie.

"I don't think she'll ever find out," Carrie replied. *And I'd be mortified if she did* she added in her mind. Josh caught her eye, and she looked away. *But I have nothing to feel guilty about!* she wanted to scream.

"Carrie," Josh said softly, placing a hand on her shoulder. She followed his gaze toward the front door. There stood Jade, peering intently at a recently posted sign that announced the gallery show.

Even looking at the sign from the back, Carrie could see that her name was featured prominently.

"What are you going to do?" Emma asked, tugging gently at Carrie's sleeve. Carrie was still staring at the sign.

"I don't have much of a choice, do I?" Carrie replied hollowly. "I've got to go talk to Jade. And to COPE. I've got to make them understand that they've got this wrong!"

"Let me come with you for moral support," Emma suggested.

"Me, too," Sam added.

"We'll all go," Josh said.

Carrie smiled at her friends. They were great—they would stand by her, no matter what. But she knew she had to do this alone. "Thanks for the offer, but I've got to handle this myself," Carrie said.

She headed resolutely for the front door.

The picketing and the chanting stopped as Carrie approached. The demonstrators seemed to be stunned that some teenager was coming out of the gallery to talk to them. They clearly hadn't expected this. Only Jade knew who Carrie was, and she stood, impassive, waiting to see what Carrie was going to say.

"I'm Carrie Alden," she said to the group. "I took some of the photographs in there."

A young man was the first person to respond. "You know why we're here!" he practically shouted at her. "This show is a farce! Your photos are a farce!"

Hot blood rushed to Carrie's face. She did not intend to get into an argument, but she didn't want some stranger calling her pictures a farce, either.

"You haven't even seen my pictures," Carrie said, trying not to sound defensive, "so how would you know?"

"I don't need to see your pictures!" he shouted. "I'm sure they show the world of the haves and not that of the have-nots."

"Why don't you show the real island?" a young mother holding a toddler by the hand challenged Carrie. "This doesn't tell the whole story!"

"Because this is a show. Because it doesn't *have* to tell the whole story!" Carrie was getting more and more angry.

"Well, that's easy for you to say, rich girl," the first young man taunted her.

"I know about this island," Carrie pleaded. "I know about the shacks and the garbage and the hungry kids. I've seen it. I've photographed it."

"Yeah, but I bet those photos aren't in

your precious exhibit, are they?" the same young man taunted.

Jade, who had remained silent during all this, finally stepped up to Carrie. "If you know what really goes on here on this island," she said quietly, "how could you let them exhibit your work in a show that tries to sweep the truth under the rug? Don't you feel any responsibility?"

"I'm responsible for my own photos!" Carrie said hotly.

"That's the lamest excuse I ever heard," the young man muttered.

Jade's face looked sad and disappointed. "Well, I guess I misjudged you after all," she said.

"Carrie!"

Carrie wheeled. May Spencer-Rumsey stood in the doorway. "Whatever are you doing talking to those people?"

"I was just trying to explain—"

"There's nothing to explain. Come inside. Now!" May said angrily.

Carrie obediently turned toward the gallery. "Rich girl," she heard someone snicker behind her. "Like a dog on a leash."

"Those demonstrators are so wrapped up in their own cause that they can't understand that politics is politics and art is art,"

May said firmly. "This should be your big moment. Now come inside and enjoy the show."

Carrie nodded and went back into the gallery. But no matter where she looked, she couldn't seem to see anything but Jade's disappointed face.

ELEVEN

"Hey, Carrie, will you drive me over to Becky's?" Ian asked the next morning as Carrie was buttering the toast.

Now, why would he want to go to Becky's and let her rag on him? Carrie thought. Ian hadn't said one word about how he was feeling since their talk after his gig. In fact, he hadn't talked much to anyone in the house at all.

"Sure," Carrie said, "if you really want me to."

"I do," Ian said. "Becky thinks bikes are dweeby," he added, which explained why he wasn't going to bike over to her house.

"Mmm, that coffee smells great," Josh said, coming into the kitchen and kissing Carrie on the cheek.

"Hi, Josh!" Chloe exclaimed. She liked Josh a lot. "Want to sit next to me?"

"I do," Josh said gravely, pouring himself a cup of coffee.

"Want to come to the beach with me today?" Chloe asked him hopefully.

Josh looked out the window at the menacing skies. The wind was kicking up, too. "It doesn't look like much of a beach day," he commented. "Besides, I'm leaving in a couple of hours."

"I'm going to drive Ian over to Becky's and then we can go do something or other before I take you to the ferry," Carrie said.

"Can I come?" Chloe said.

Carrie looked at Josh. She was hoping Claudia would wake up and volunteer to take the little girl for a few hours so she could spend a little time alone with Josh before he left. "Uh, we'll see," Carrie said.

"That always means no," Chloe sighed. She looked out the window at the tree branches being whipped around wildly. "Is this the hurricane?" she asked fearfully.

"No, honey," Carrie assured her. "It's just some wind and rain."

Carrie turned on the radio near her bed as she dressed, listening for an update on Hurricane Julius. The last she'd heard, the storm wasn't expected to hit the island, but it really *did* look nasty out.

"And now a weather update on Hurricane Julius. Currently the hurricane is located two hundred miles due east of Cape May, New Jersey, and is zeroing in on the New Jersey coast, with landfall expected at Toms River in about fifteen hours. Rain should overspread the entire northeast after the hurricane passes over land and begins to disintegrate. Julius currently packs top winds of one hundred ten miles per hour."

Well, good, thought Carrie. *We're just in for some rain, then.* Between thinking about what had happened at the gallery the night before, and worrying about her relationships with Josh and Billy, she *definitely* did not have the energy to worry about a hurricane!

Carrie helped Chloe dress, then the two of them went downstairs. Josh was already all packed, and was playing Nintendo with Ian. There was no sign of Claudia or Graham. *Oh, well,* Carrie sighed inwardly, *I'll just have to take Chloe along for the big goodbye. Maybe it will even make it easier.*

Ian assured Carrie that he'd called Becky and okayed their coming over, so they all piled into the van and drove to the Jacobses' house. They found Becky, Allie, and Sam in the den listening to a Garth Brooks CD.

"I'm shameless!" Becky and Allie sang along with Garth, throwing their arms out dramatically.

"Hey, guys!" Sam greeted them, turning the music down. "Nice surprise."

"Didn't Becky tell you Ian called?" Carrie asked.

Becky put her hands on her hips. "Ian didn't call me," she said.

Carrie stared at Ian.

"I lied," Ian said in a low voice. "I thought she'd tell me not to come."

"You thought right," Becky said. "I hope no one saw you drive up," she added.

Sam gave Becky a look of disgust. "Honestly, Becky, you really can be a brat, you know?"

Unexpectedly, Becky blushed.

"I just wanted to tell you something," Ian said.

"We can leave," Carrie offered. "I mean, we can go in the kitchen or something."

"No, I want to say this in front of everyone," Ian insisted.

"Even me?" Chloe asked.

Ian ignored her. "The thing is, I know my band wasn't very good the other day."

"You can say that again," Allie muttered under her breath.

Sam kicked her in the shin. "Go on, Ian," she encouraged.

"Well, no one starts out being good at anything," Ian said, staring at the ground. "Besides, industrial music is new, so it's hard for people to understand it."

"But I told you," Becky said with exasperation, "all you have to do is to sing your dad's stuff. Then you'd be really excellent!"

Ian looked Becky straight in the eye. "I'm not my dad, okay?" he said loudly. "No matter what anyone thinks, I'm an artist, and artists follow their own vision, not anyone else's. So if you don't like it, Becky, too bad." Ian took a deep breath. "Well, that's all I wanted to say," he finished self-consciously.

Carrie grinned at Ian. She was *so* proud of him!

Josh put his hand out to the boy. "Put it there, my man," he said, shaking Ian's hand.

Becky stood up and walked over to Ian. "Let me get this straight. You think that noise you make is art? And you're going to keep doing it?"

"Yep," Ian said firmly.

"Oh," was Becky's reply.

"I'll go wait in the van," Ian said, and walked out the door.

"That is a very cool kid," Sam told Becky. "I hope you're smart enough to realize it."

Becky looked thoughtful for a moment. "Do you think he might, like . . . grow a few inches?" she asked hopefully.

Everyone laughed. "It's a good bet," Carrie answered.

Becky looked at her sister. "Let's go out to the van and talk to him," she said.

"I thought you didn't want to be seen with him ever again!" Allie reminded her.

"Well, I changed my mind," Becky said, tossing her hair. "Come on."

Allie sighed and followed Becky out the front door.

"Amazing," Sam said, shaking her head. "You guys want anything to eat or drink?" she offered.

"Do you have a cookie?" Chloe asked shyly.

"Yes, I have a cookie." Sam laughed. "Come to the kitchen, you fox-of-the-future, you."

Sam took Chloe's hand and they skipped into the kitchen. "Make yourselves at home!" Sam called back to Carrie and Josh.

Josh put his arms around Carrie. "You've

had a really positive influence on the kid, do you know that?"

"Thanks," Carrie said. *Not that I always follow my own good advice*, she added in her head.

"We didn't get to spend very much time alone while I was here," Josh murmured into Carrie's hair.

"Well, I was working," Carrie explained lamely. She knew she'd deliberately tried *not* to be alone with Josh too much. Her feelings were just too confusing.

Josh kissed Carrie's eyes, her nose, then tenderly kissed her lips. Carrie kissed him back. It felt good. It felt right. Encouraged by this, Josh kissed her passionately, pressing her closely against him until they were both breathless.

Am I doing this because he's leaving and it's safe? Carrie asked herself wildly. *Or maybe I'm just losing my mind completely!*

"Oh, Carrie," Josh groaned in her ear. "I've missed you so much."

"But we've been together for days!" Carrie answered playfully.

"You know what I mean," Josh said in a low voice.

Red alert! Dangerous ground! An alarm went off in Carrie's head. Josh had been her

171

first lover. They'd loved each other very much. And they'd been careful and responsible. But how could Carrie continue that kind of a relationship with him when she wasn't committed to him anymore? She couldn't! "I told you how I feel about that," Carrie said, taking a step backwards.

"How can you turn it on and off like that?" Josh asked in frustration.

"Josh, I told you—" Carrie began.

"I know, I know," Josh said, "the I-want-to-be-friends bit. Well, that was more than a friendly kiss just now, and you know it."

"You're right," Carrie said quietly. "I shouldn't have done it."

"What I want to know is," Josh said evenly, "do you pull this same crap with Billy?"

"I . . . what?" Carrie asked. Why was Josh getting so angry now, just when he was about to leave? Had it been building up all this time?

"Carrie, are you sleeping with him?" Josh asked.

"Well, Chloe, here are three cookies, so don't be surprised if you don't feel like eating any lunch," Sam said, coming back into the den with the little girl in hand.

"Three *big* cookies!" Chloe corrected her.

172

Sam looked from Carrie's face to Josh's and back again. "Oops," she said. "Maybe Chloe and I should go find something to color . . . or something."

"No, we're leaving," Carrie said. "Come on, Chloe." Josh followed her.

"Hey, by the way, I had a fantastic time last night," Sam told Carrie. "That guy with the European accent asked for my phone number."

"Great," Carrie said, taking Chloe by the hand.

"So I'll call you later," Sam called as Carrie walked out the door.

When they got to the van, Becky and Allie were sitting on either side of Ian in the back seat, and appeared to be vying for his attention.

"Carrie," Becky said when Carrie opened the door, "don't you think backup singers for the Zit Men is a really good idea?"

"You can't sing. *I* can sing," Allie told her sister.

"I'm so sure." Becky snorted. "You sound like a sick frog."

"You are so full of it!" Allie yelled back at her sister. "I sing a hell of a lot better than you do!"

"Well, I don't know if we really want

backup singers, anyway," Ian said. "But I'll let you know."

The twins climbed out of the van and waved good-bye as Carrie pulled the van out of the driveway. She could see in her rear-view mirror that Ian had a huge grin on his face. Now if only her mood were half as good as his was, things would be fine.

Fortunately Graham and Claudia were awake when Carrie drove Ian and Chloe home, and Claudia said she could leave to spend some time alone with Josh before his ferry left.

They drove to the dunes and parked in a secluded spot behind the largest dune they could find. Then they talked for what felt like hours, but nothing seemed to get resolved. Josh wanted their old relationship back, but the very thought of it made Carrie feel as if there were a noose around her neck.

"It's just that . . . I love you, Carrie," Josh said softly, his voice choked with emotion. "I know you're the person I want to spend my life with."

"But how can you know that?" Carrie asked him passionately. "We're only nineteen years old!"

"I'm young, I'm not stupid," Josh said. "There was a time when you used to say you knew it, too."

He was right. All through their senior year Carrie had been convinced that she'd marry Josh and they'd be blissfully happy together. But was wanting to experience something of life before settling down such a crime?

"I'm just not ready for that," Carrie explained. "I think I need to concentrate on school and my photography now, you know?"

"You mean hobnobbing with the rich and famous, don't you?" Josh asked bitterly.

"No, I don't!" Carrie shot back, truly hurt. Surely Josh knew her better than that!

"You're right, I'm just pissed," Josh said.

"I'm even thinking about doing some volunteer work for COPE," Carrie said defensively.

"Okay, fine," Josh said.

"It's like May said: politics is politics, and art is art," Carrie decreed.

Josh looked at her with a raised eyebrow. "Yeah, well, if you believe that, why do you sound so defensive?"

"I don't!" Carrie shot back.

There was silence in the van. They

couldn't seem to talk about their relationship, and they couldn't seem to talk about her photography. Carrie sighed. They used to be able to talk about everything.

"Wow, the sky is getting really dark," Josh remarked. "What time is it?"

Carrie checked her watch. "Time for your ferry," she said, starting the van. As she drove toward the ferry slip, Carrie realized how menacing the weather looked. Between being parked behind the dune and being lost in their own conversation, neither of them had noticed.

"Turn on the radio. We'll see if there's a storm update," Josh urged. "This sky looks awfully dark."

Carrie flipped on the radio to the all-news station. She heard a familiar high-pitched whine, followed by a recorded voice instructing listeners to tune to a different station. "Omigod," she cried, "it's the Emergency Broadcast System. And I don't think this is a test."

Josh punched buttons until the radio was tuned to the proper station. They listened, transfixed, as the announcer read the same message over and over again.

"This is an emergency advisory from the National Weather Service for the Massachusetts, New Hampshire, and Maine coastlines. Hurricane Julius has changed course, and is approaching your area at a speed of thirty-five miles per hour.

"Please make all appropriate preparations. This is a hurricane warning. Listen to the instructions of emergency officials. Do not go outdoors during the storm. Stay away from low ground. Tides are expected to be ten to fifteen feet above normal. Again, listen to the instructions of local emergency officials. All ferry traffic has been halted by the Coast Guard. This message will be repeated until the next advisory is issued."

Carrie and Josh looked out at the rapidly darkening skies. The winds were beginning to pick up noticeably, and they saw sand beginning to blow off the top of the dunes.

"We'd better get out of here," Carrie said worriedly, her knuckles white against the steering wheel.

"Where to?" Josh asked.

"Back to Graham and Claudia's," Carrie answered, gunning the engine and turning the van around. "I think you can forget about the ferry. Those kids must be scared to death." She remembered Ian scaring Chloe with an exaggerated story about how a hurricane could tear a house into a million tiny pieces. *I hope he* was *exaggerating*, she thought grimly.

All the way back to the Templetons' house, they saw an occasional emergency vehicle with flashing lights out on the roads, and people working feverishly outside their homes, boarding up windows and stowing outdoor furniture.

"This island is not equipped for this," Carrie said with anxiety. "There are only ten police officers and three police cars, and there's only one fire truck and two ambulances."

When they pulled into the Templetons' driveway, Carrie and Josh saw Claudia, Graham, and Ian hard at work battening down the hatches. Claudia waved at them with relief as they approached.

"Thank goodness!" Claudia said, her sleeves rolled up and her long hair blowing in the wind. "I had no idea what happened to you."

"We're here," Carrie replied, getting out of the van. "Now, what can we do to help?"

Carrie and Josh pitched in at the back of the house, bringing in all the outdoor furniture and sculpture and nailing plywood—which Graham luckily had a good supply of in his workroom—across the sliding glass doors. Then Carrie went upstairs and put X's of masking tape across all the windows, as Claudia told her to do.

"It won't stop the windows from breaking," she said, "but at least the glass won't fly everywhere."

Finally, they finished. The wind was up to forty-five miles per hour. Chloe was staring up at her father with eyes huge with fear. He comforted her as best he could, but even Chloe seemed to know that there were some things even Daddy might not be able to protect her from. The Templeton family, Carrie, and Josh huddled inside the house, waiting. There was nothing left to do but wait for the worst and pray that it wouldn't come.

TWELVE

"Ian, come away from the window!" Graham yelled at his son.

"But there's a car driving up, Dad!" Ian said, peering out.

A moment later there was a knock at the door. Graham handed Chloe to Claudia and went to open the door.

"Hi, is Carrie here?" It was Kurt Ackerman in a yellow rain slicker, his wet hair blowing wildly.

Carrie ran to the door and pulled Kurt inside. "What are you *doing* here?"

"Don't you know it's dangerous to be out driving?" Claudia asked.

"Listen, Carrie, I need your help," Kurt said. There was an intensity on his face that Carrie had never seen before. "The people from COPE are sandbagging near the lane and trying to get everyone out of those shacks. We need all the help we can get."

"Kurt, you can't expect Carrie to go out in this!" Claudia cried.

"There isn't much time," Kurt said, staring at Carrie. "What little those people have in this world will be completely destroyed, Carrie. They could die."

"I—I can't . . ." Carrie stammered.

"Smart decision," Claudia said approvingly.

But it was as if a light bulb had flashed on in Carrie's head. May Spencer-Rumsey had told her the same thing. Smart decision. Well, maybe *smart* was a relative term. Maybe sometimes you had to be courageous, instead.

Kurt turned around and headed for the front door, but Carrie's voice stopped him.

"Wait," she called. "I'm coming with you."

"But that's crazy!" Graham protested.

"And I am, too," Josh said, staring at Carrie. She grinned up into his determined face.

"Let's go," Kurt said. And all three headed out into the storm.

They climbed into Kurt's borrowed four-wheel-drive vehicle and Kurt drove as quickly as he possibly could toward the poverty-stricken community dodging falling tree branches and even once a downed power line. The wind was blowing so hard that the torrential rain was falling not down but *sideways*.

Carrie and Josh sat, white-knuckled, in the back seat of the jeep, since Kurt had all sorts of shovels and other equipment next to him. Their hands were clenched together out of fear.

"Jeez," Kurt yelled. "Look at that!" He pointed to the snapped trunk of a maple tree along the side of the road.

"What if we had been under it!" Carrie wailed, truly scared.

"Chance you gotta take," Kurt said grimly. "I'm going as fast as I can." The car radio kept repeating the same National Weather Service advisory over and over again.

"Rubie told me all about Hurricane Donna," Kurt said, steering with both hands firmly gripping the wheel. "She said the island was cut off from the mainland for three days. Not my idea of a good time. Look! There's the turnoff."

Kurt made a sharp right turn, and instantly found his traction gone.

"Damn," he swore. "It's the mud. No drainage here. Guess we'll four-wheel-drive it from here on in." He popped a few switches inside the Jeep, put his foot on the accelerator, and the Jeep started to make progress again.

"Double damn," Kurt uttered viciously. A small downed tree blocked the road up ahead. He slowed to a stop.

"Okay, Josh," he said, turning to the back seat, "let's get to work."

"You mean try to move it?" Josh asked.

"That's right. Let's go!"

"I'm helping, too," Carrie decided.

The three of them fought their way through the wind and rain to the tree. But try as they might, they couldn't move it an inch.

"Back to the Jeep!" Kurt yelled to Josh and Carrie over the wind. They leaned into the wind as they walked back and practically fell into the Jeep, totally out of breath.

"No choice," Kurt said, breathing heavily. "No choice. We've got to get through. Put on your seatbelts," he instructed Josh and Carrie. "We're going over it."

When Josh and Carrie nodded that they were buckled in, Kurt gunned the engine. *Whap! Whap! Whap! Whap!* The Jeep crashed through the branches of the fallen tree and ran over the trunk.

"We're through!" Kurt exulted. "And there's COPE!"

Dead ahead, Carrie could make out through the rain about six or seven other vans and about twenty people in yellow slickers. All the people were hard at work, enduring the most lashing rain and howling wind any of them had ever seen.

Carrie gulped hard. She felt fear in every inch of her body. *I want to be doing that?* Carrie asked herself. *Oh no*, she answered, *you're not changing your mind now. Just get to it.*

"Okay, let's get to work!" Kurt said. "See those people filling sandbags? That's where we're going to start," he said, motioning to a group of about eight COPE members and a dozen local residents who were shoveling dirt into sacks as fast as they could and placing the filled sandbags along the banks of a creek that now resembled a rushing river.

Carrie, Josh, and Kurt jumped out of the Jeep and ran over to the group, Kurt pausing to take some shovels out of the front seat. They worked like demons.

Carrie felt painful blisters developing on her palms. *Forget about the blisters*, she told herself. *If we don't sandbag this creek, these people are going to be flooded out. Permanently.*

The rain poured down. It was two steps forward and one step back, as water sometimes poured through holes in their makeshift levee. But each time, they were able to seal the breach.

"Okay!" a drenched man in his forties yelled. *He's the leader*, Carrie thought. *I can barely hear him over the wind.* "We've got to get these people out of here and to the fire station in town! Come on!" The man starting running as best he could toward the tumbledown shacks.

Kurt, Carrie, and Josh followed him.

"What's he doing?" Carrie shouted over the wind to Kurt.

"No emergency vehicles are coming down here," Kurt shouted back. "We've got to evacuate these people ourselves. Otherwise they die!"

At the first shack, the man found a young mother, her two young children, and a dog. He pointed to Kurt.

"Ackerman!" he shouted. "Get these people out!" And to the family, "Follow him!"

Josh and Carrie raced to get the kids. Kurt grabbed the dog in his arms.

"Careful!" the woman yelled to Carrie as

she went to lift the little girl. "A lamp fell on her arm. I think her wrist is broken."

"I'll be really careful," Carrie said, speaking softly to the petrified little girl, who nodded mutely.

"You put your good arm around my shoulder, and I'll carry you out." Carrie lifted the girl gently.

"Good," Kurt said, nodding at Carrie. "See that black Chevy out there? That's where we're headed. Now, run!"

Carrie, Josh, and Kurt ran as quickly as they could to the van. Rain pelted their faces. Everyone was soaked in a matter of seconds. Carrie carefully helped the little girl into the back of the van. Josh and the little boy piled in back through the other door, while the mother sat in front with the dog on her lap.

"All here? Good! Now, hold on!" Kurt started the engine and headed back down the road to town. *It's raining even harder!* Carrie thought. *And the mud's a lot thicker. What if we get stuck here?* Carrie tried to banish the thought from her mind, but several times it seemed as if Kurt was on the verge of getting mired in the mud. The kids in back started wailing, the little girl screaming that her wrist hurt.

"It'll be okay, baby," her mother said, trying to comfort the girl. "Hush, now."

It seemed like ages before Kurt came to the main road and made the turn toward downtown and the shelter at the fire station.

"It looks like a war zone out there!" Josh whispered, not wanting to upset the kids further. But he was right—many of the stores had broken windows, and several parked cars had been crushed by fallen trees. And the storm showed no signs of letting up.

Kurt pulled into the fire station, where the volunteer firefighters had set up an emergency shelter. The fire truck was gone—out on emergency duty, obviously—but several volunteers were there.

"Get those kids here!" one of them shouted as the Chevy slowed.

"There's two of them," Kurt said through the window, breathless. "More coming right behind."

"I don't know if you're brave or crazy," one of the volunteers told Kurt as she helped the kids inside.

"Both," Kurt muttered, turning around to see what else he could do to help.

But there wasn't much for him to do. The volunteers handed out dry clothes and a blanket to each person who came in and gave them a cup of hot cocoa. Kurt, Carrie, and Josh slumped down gratefully on a few nearby chairs and watched the other COPE vehicles pull in and unload their evacuees.

"Pretty wild, huh, guys?" Kurt said, a smile playing over his exhausted face.

"And how!" Josh said, closing his eyes.

"You can say that again!" Carrie chimed in. She was as tired as she'd ever been in her life. Muscles that she hadn't even known she had ached and ached.

"Well, Carrie," Kurt said grimly, "you should be glad you got those photos of those shacks when you did. Because tomorrow they may find them floating someplace off the coast of Rhode Island."

Carrie frowned. Something about what Kurt said bothered her. *Photos*, she thought. *Photos*.

May Spencer-Rumsey's voice came back to her as clear as day. At the exhibit the previous evening, May had told Carrie that she was going to escort David and Edine Frohman back to Boston in the morning, and that they might talk some business on the way. She had promised to call Carrie as soon as she returned.

And then it hit her. *There's no one at*

May's house! Carrie thought wildly. *It sits right out there on that point. And—*

"Omigod!" Carrie shouted, jumping to her feet. "May's photography collection! It'll be destroyed! We've got to save it!"

"What are you talking about?" Josh and Kurt said at the same time. They were too tired to move.

Carrie quickly explained to them about May's extensive collection.

"No sweat, Carrie," Kurt said, "She's so rich, she's probably got them insured fifteen times over."

"Don't you get it?" Carrie screamed. "You can't replace art. Who knows if there are other copies anywhere! We have to do something!"

A small group of COPE members gathered around Carrie and Kurt. Carrie recognized a man and a woman who had been among the picketers at the Sunset Gallery exhibit.

"Hey, count me out," the woman said. "I'll go out in this storm to save lives. But not photos. Correction. Not *that* woman's photos," she said, contempt dripping from her voice.

"*That* woman," Carrie snapped back, "didn't take those pictures. Some great artists did. *That* woman is going to die someday. But those pictures deserve to live!"

Silence. Not even a halfhearted retort.

"Come on, Josh," Carrie said, motioning to Josh to stand up. "Kurt? Come on. We're going to go save those pictures."

Kurt and Josh looked at each other. They were still exhausted. Neither stood up.

"Kurt? Josh? *Come on!*" Carrie started walking toward the Chevy Kurt had driven in.

Josh and Kurt stood up slowly and followed her.

"Ackerman!"

Kurt turned around. The COPE leader was calling him.

"Ackerman," he said, "I'm not letting you go out to Winterhaven alone." He looked at the other COPE members. "I'm going with you. And any of you who care to come"—he motioned to his group—"would be appreciated."

Slowly, everyone stood up. They were all going back out into the storm.

Following a harrowing drive, the COPE motorcade arrived at Winterhaven. Just as Carrie suspected, no one there had taken even the most elementary storm precautions. Windows were smashed open all over the mansion, and ocean water from the storm surge lapped at the back door.

"Carrie, you've got to lead the way," Kurt said after pulling the Chevy as close to the front door as he could. "You know where everything is."

Carrie quickly took charge. "Okay, here's what we need to do," she replied. "We've got to get those photos off the walls and into a waterproof area of the house. There's a storage room upstairs that has no windows. It'll be perfect."

The front door was locked, but Kurt and Carrie climbed through a busted window and opened it from the inside. Then Carrie led the COPE contingent into the mansion and right to the room with the photography. She opened the door.

Whoosh! A torrent of water rushed out at the group. Carrie was knocked off her feet, but Josh caught her from behind. "Watch out!" she shouted to the others. People grabbed quickly onto walls and doors to anchor themselves as the water flooded past.

"Everyone okay?" she asked, looking behind her. The people nodded.

"Just be careful getting those pictures off

the walls," Kurt yelled to the group. "Get 'em down, then follow Carrie upstairs."

The COPE members followed Carrie's plan exactly. Within a half-hour, all the photos were in the upstairs storage room, which Carrie tried to waterproof as best she could.

"Carrie!" Josh yelled upstairs to her.

"Yes?" she shouted back.

"You done?" he asked. "It's starting to flood down here!"

"Just about!" Carrie answered, wrapping plastic sheeting around the last couple of picture frames.

"Then let's get out of here! Now!"

Carrie took one last look at the David Frohman photo nearest her, then walked resolutely to the door without looking back.

That's the best I can do, she thought. *I only hope it's good enough.*

THIRTEEN

Carrie woke up the next morning wondering if she'd dreamed the whole thing—the hurricane, the harrowing trip through the streets to rescue the shacks' residents, the trip back to May Spencer-Rumsey's house to try and save the photographs. But when she lifted her throbbing hands out from under the blankets and looked at the raw blisters on her palms, she knew it was no dream.

"Hi. Are you awake?" Josh asked softly, sticking his head around the door.

"My whole body hurts," Carrie groaned.

"I guess you're not used to hand-to-hand combat with a hurricane," Josh said.

Carrie swung her feet to the floor. "How bad is it out?" she asked anxiously. When they'd driven home the night before, it had been pitch-black outside. Now, in the light, they could grimly assess the damage.

"Not too bad around here," Josh told her.

Carrie went to the window and peered out. She could see fallen tree branches and debris in the pool, but all in all, it didn't look that bad.

"What about the rest of the island?" Carrie asked worriedly.

"The local news report just said there's some very heavy damage on the ocean side," Josh said. "Homes totaled, power lines down, roads washed out. And three people were killed."

"God, that's horrible!" Carrie cried.

"There's a volunteer cleanup crew over there now," Josh said.

"I'll throw on some clothes and we'll go," Carrie decided, heading for the bathroom. "That is, if you want to come with me," she amended, turning back to him.

"I'm with you, Carrie," Josh said quietly. "You know that."

Carrie showered quickly, letting the hot water loosen her sore muscles. She bandaged her blisters, threw on some jeans and a sweatshirt, and headed downstairs.

"No one's up?" Carrie asked when she saw Josh alone in the kitchen.

"Nope. It's early."

"I know they'll understand if I go," Carrie

said. "I'll just leave a note." Carrie scribbled quickly and grabbed muffins for her and Josh, and they sped out the door.

As Carrie drove the van toward the ocean, the damage grew more and more obvious. The power was still out over most of the island, and it was clear that certain sections of Sunset Island had been badly torn up by Hurricane Julius.

Carrie saw, in the space of a bare quarter-mile, a mobile home flipped over on its side, three automobiles completely staved in by fallen trees, several downed telephone and power lines, and many, many areas still badly flooded. Several other large trees had been completely uprooted in people's yards, and she saw that the chimney of another house had been blown off completely. The more she saw, the more anxious she was about the poorest neighborhoods. If these beautiful, well-built homes had sustained this kind of damage, what had happened to the dilapidated shacks?

"Oh, no," Carrie breathed when they turned down the unmarked lane. Destruction was everywhere. Many of the shacks had been completely flattened. Those that stood were badly damaged.

"There's Kurt," Josh said, pointing ahead

of them. A group of people were pulling debris off a rusted school bus. Two police cars and the island's fire truck surrounded them.

"Hi," Carrie said to Kurt, touching his arm softly. He turned around. There was a terrible look of pain and exhaustion in his eyes.

"Hi, Carrie, Josh," Kurt said. "They just found Sam Webber in this bus," he added. Carrie remembered that Jade had mentioned Sam, an old man who drank too much and lived on the street. All the folks in the area sort of took care of him, but he had no home.

"He stayed in this bus in the hurricane?" Carrie asked, horrified. "But I thought we checked everywhere."

"He must have crawled in after that," Kurt said.

"Is he . . . ?" Carrie asked. She couldn't make herself finish the question.

"He's alive," Kurt told her. "But he's got two broken legs and a lot of lacerations."

"Poor old guy," Josh said.

Kurt ran his hand through his hair and rubbed his red-rimmed eyes. "It's just not right, you know? In this world you either have or have not, and this little island is no exception."

"Kurt, Russell says to go house to house and make sure no one else got caught anywhere," a familiar well-bred female voice said.

"Emma!" Carrie cried. She was surprised and happy to see her friend.

"Hi," Emma said, giving Carrie a warm hug. "Kurt called and asked me to come help," she explained shyly. Carrie could see how happy Emma was that Kurt had called her.

"I'll go with you," Carrie volunteered.

"I'll stay and help over here," Josh said, and joined the group clearing the heavy debris from the bus and the road.

"Be careful," Kurt warned them.

"And don't touch downed power lines or anything that looks unstable," the head of COPE called over to them.

"Kurt told me you and Josh were here all last night," Emma said as they walked over to the first still-standing shack. "It was really brave of you."

"It didn't feel brave," Carrie mused. "It just felt . . . I don't know, like something I had to do." Carrie told Emma about going to May's house to save the priceless photo-

199

graphs. "And the amazing thing is," Carrie marveled, "that the people from COPE went with me to help, even after what happened at the gallery."

"It sort of makes you want to help them even more, doesn't it?" Emma asked.

"It sure makes me respect them, I'll tell you that," Carrie said firmly.

Gingerly the girls walked up what was left of the front steps of a half-destroyed shack.

"Hello?" Emma called out. "Is anyone here?"

"God, look at this," Carrie breathed, staring at the debris that littered the floor. Garbage, wood fragments and shards of glass mingled with the few possessions of the people who had lived there—some broken dishes, an old doll, a bare mattress.

And somehow, a small photograph remained tacked to the one wall that still stood. Carrie looked closer. In the photo were four small children and a worn-looking woman smiling tentatively at the camera.

"That's the little boy I photographed," Carrie whispered, recognizing the sad-faced boy. *This must be where he lives— correction*, she thought. *Where he lived.*

"Hey, you girls come out of there!" a deep male voice yelled to them.

Carrie and Emma went out onto the porch. A gruff-looking police officer was standing in front of the house.

"We were told to search," Carrie said.

"Well, you were told wrong," the officer said tersely. "You could get hurt."

"We plan to be extremely careful," Emma said in her most proper voice.

The officer reacted to Emma's cultured voice immediately, apparently figuring she was one of the rich summer people and not just some local COPE volunteer. "Yes, ma'am," he said with deference. "But we could have all kinds of insurance problems if you got hurt."

The officer gave them both a hand and helped them down the porch. "With all due respect, ladies," he said, "there's nothing you can do here."

"He means there's nothing they'll let us do," Carrie said under her breath to Emma as they walked back to the group.

"They're making all of us leave," Kurt told the girls with disgust when they reached him.

"But why won't they let us help?" Carrie cried.

"They said it's some insurance regulation," Kurt said, "but that's bull. I think it might have something to do with *that*." He pointed to a TV news van that was just pulling into the lane.

"We have to rope this area off," a police officer told them. "You will all have to move."

"Sometimes you can't fight city hall," Kurt muttered as they walked toward their vehicles.

"I'd like to drive by Winterhaven," Carrie said to Josh when they reached the van. She turned around to call to Kurt and Emma. "Do you want to drive over to Winterhaven?"

Kurt shook his head. "I'm going back to help the people staying at the fire station," he called to her.

"Me, too," Emma said, taking Kurt's arm lovingly. "Good luck!" she added, holding up crossed fingers.

Carrie drove silently to Winterhaven, scared of what kind of destruction she might find. *Because of its location, that house was just so vulnerable*, she thought. *Maybe moving the photos was just an exercise in futility*. She wondered if somehow May thought that being rich could protect her and her property from anything—even nature.

"Well, it's still standing," Carrie said with relief as they approached the mansion.

"Part of it," Josh corrected glumly as they drove closer. Now they could see that the wall closest to the ocean was gone. Carrie could only imagine what the inside of the house looked like.

They parked in the driveway—and this time there was no uniformed servant to park the car. Carrie peered in through a broken window. "May?" she called. "Anybody here?"

"There are two cars in the garage, so someone is probably here," Josh called to Carrie as he peered through a narrow crack in the garage door.

"Yeah, but who knows how many cars she owns?" Carrie said. She knocked on the front door as hard as she could. "May?" she called again.

Miraculously, the door opened. There stood a white-faced May Spencer-Rumsey. "Carrie, what are you doing here?" she asked in a dead-sounding voice.

"We came to see if everything was okay here," Carrie said. She and Josh stepped inside the hall.

"I just got back," May said. "It's terrible. The back of the house is completely destroyed," she said. "But worse than that, someone broke in and stole my entire photo collection!"

Then Carrie realized that May had no idea the photos had been moved and might actually be safe. "No, that's not what happened," Carrie said, and quickly explained about moving the photos.

May's face lit up with hope. Without a word she turned around and headed for the storage room upstairs, with Carrie and Josh right behind her.

May opened the door. The three of them stood there staring at the photos, which were untouched, unhurt, perfect.

"Thank God!" May cried fervently, tears coming to her eyes. She turned around and hugged Carrie. "How ever did you do it?"

Carrie explained how she, Josh, Kurt, and the members of COPE had battled to save the photographs.

May shook her head in amazement. "That is an incredible story," she said. "I can't thank you enough, Carrie. I wish there was something I could do to show you what this means to me."

"Maybe there is," Carrie said slowly. "Josh and I couldn't have done it without the people from COPE. They're really good people, May. You could help them."

"All right," May said finally. "I'll make a donation. Let me get my checkbook."

"That's a start," Carrie agreed, "but what they really want is your recognition. If you would just consider putting some of those other photos in the book, I really think the better-off people on the island would begin to acknowledge the problems COPE is trying to address."

"I'm sorry, Carrie," May sighed, "but I can't do that. I don't agree with their methods and I don't support their causes."

"But you said—" Carrie began.

"I'll make the donation," May interrupted, "because you asked me to, and because they helped save the photos. But I dare say they don't believe in the things I believe in, any more than I believe in the things they believe in."

"They believe in justice!" Carrie cried.

"They believe in a free ride," May corrected.

Carrie looked at Josh for moral support. He took her hand and squeezed it, but there was nothing he could say.

"Come downstairs, you two, and I will

write a check for COPE, but that's all I will do."

Carrie and Josh followed May downstairs and stood there while she wrote out the check. *Well, COPE can certainly use the money,* Carrie thought. *But it's so easy for her just to write a check. The money doesn't mean anything to her. Those people risked their lives to save her art!*

May handed Carrie the check, and suddenly Carrie knew what she had to do. "May," she said, "I've changed my mind. I don't want my photos used in your book unless you include some that show the not-so-perfect side of this island, too."

May stared at Carrie. Out of the corner of Carrie's eye she could see Josh's face. She didn't know if she'd ever seen anyone look that proud before.

"Oh, Carrie, dear, you don't mean that," May said. "You're just upset."

"I am upset," Carrie agreed, "but I do mean it."

"But this is such a meaningless gesture," May said earnestly. "Having your photos published wouldn't hurt your friends at COPE, would it?"

"Maybe not," Carrie allowed. "But when I think of what they did for you, and what you're unwilling to do for them, I just can't go through with it."

"I wish you'd change your mind," May said, getting up.

"I wish *you* would," Carrie countered.

"It's like I told you," May said sadly, "art is art and politics is politics. I'm sorry."

"I guess I just don't believe that," Carrie said thoughtfully. "I want to take pictures that can change things, not just pictures that look good."

May smiled at her. "You're very talented, Carrie, and very young."

Carrie didn't smile back. "You've told me that more than once," she said, "and it's really condescending." Carrie couldn't believe the way she was talking to May but she couldn't stop herself. "You know, I have a grandmother in Florida, and she went to Washington to protest the building of a nuclear power plant," Carrie continued. "I have a feeling she'd agree with my decision, and *she's* seventy-four."

"Touché," May said, a glint of respect in her eyes.

"Thank you for the check," Carrie said stiffly, and turned on her heel. Josh was right beside her.

"Good luck, Carrie," May called as Carrie walked toward the front door.

But Carrie didn't answer. She just kept walking.

Carrie and Josh rode in silence most of the way back to the Templetons' house.

"So, am I the biggest fool who ever lived?" Carrie finally asked Josh.

"Maybe," Josh said with a teasing smile, "but you sure are *my* kind of fool."

"It's funny," Carrie mused, "but I don't feel like there was a right or wrong answer to this. That's what made it so hard to know what to do."

"I know what you mean," Josh said, nodding.

"When Sam was telling me to go ahead and let May include my work in the book, and then use the money I got to help COPE, that really made sense to me!" Carrie confessed. "And I don't think it would have been wrong, either. But I think it would have been wrong for *me*, you know?"

Josh reached over and caressed Carrie's neck. "Sometimes you just have to listen to your heart," he said softly.

Carrie gave him a grateful smile and turned into the Templetons' driveway.

And there, in the driveway, leaning against the Flirts' van, was Billy Sampson.

"Is that who I think it is?" Josh asked Carrie.

"It's Billy." Carrie gulped, her heart pounding in her chest. *What is he doing here?* Billy had visited her a couple of times at Yale, but Josh had successfully avoided actually meeting him.

Carrie parked and walked over to Billy, Josh next to her. She awkwardly introduced them to each other, and they shook hands.

"I'm going in to pack," Josh told Carrie, pointedly kissing her before going in the house.

"Bad timing, huh?" Billy asked Carrie.

"Sort of," Carrie agreed.

"Our phone is still out, and I wanted to come see if you were okay," Billy said. "I figured Josh was already gone."

"You figured wrong. He got stuck here because of the storm," Carrie said. Her feelings were still all jumbled up. One part of her was glad that Billy cared enough to come check on her; another part of her was just embarrassed and didn't want to see Josh hurt; and still another part of her was angry at Billy for ignoring her all this time.

"Well, I'm glad to see you're okay," Billy

said. "I guess I should go." He turned around and opened the door of the van.

"Billy, wait," Carrie said, her hand on his arm. "Are all the Flirts okay? And your house?"

"Every single one of our windows got broken, but we're all fine," Billy said. "It was pretty hairy there for a while, though. That house we rent is real old. It sure rattled and rolled when those wind gusts hit it."

Carrie tried to think of something to say. Suddenly she felt tongue-tied and shy, like she had felt when she first met Billy.

"So . . . I'll be going," Billy said.

"I just want to know why you didn't even call me all this time," Carrie finally blurted out.

"You had company," Billy said pointedly.

"So?" Carrie asked. "You didn't care."

Billy faced Carrie, a muscle working in his jaw. "Look, Carrie, I don't know what you want. You invited the guy to visit. That's cool. It was your decision. But you can't have it both ways—him here, me on a string."

"No need to worry about that," Carrie shot back. "I saw you at the Play Café with Diana De Witt. I left before you saw me."

"I wasn't *with* her, I was *talking* to her," Billy corrected. "There's a difference."

"Not to her," Carrie mumbled.

"Believe it or not, I have a mind of my own," Billy said with a wry look on his face. "Meaning I have no interest in Diana."

Billy turned around and stepped into the van. He stared at Carrie out the window. "Should I call you?"

"Do you want to call me?" Carrie countered.

"I got some great shots of you in that blue bathing suit on the beach," Billy said softly. "But, you know, they just don't compare to the real thing."

A flush of happiness poured through Carrie. Her face lit up in a grin. "I'd like to see them."

"Tomorrow?" Billy asked, starting the van.

"Tomorrow," Carrie agreed. She waved to Billy as he drove off.

Okay, Carrie, she told herself, taking a deep breath, *time to go in and face Josh.* She found him in the guest room, sitting on the bed next to his suitcase. *That's right,* Carrie thought. *He didn't need to pack at all. He was all packed yesterday.*

211

She sat down next to him and took his hand.

"Don't," he said, pulling his hand away.

"I didn't tell him to come over," Carrie said softly.

"But you're glad he did." Josh sounded miserable.

Carrie couldn't answer. It was all so confusing! And just as with the decision she'd had to make about the photography book, nothing seemed completely right or completely wrong. All she could do was search her heart for what was right for her.

"Josh," she finally said quietly. "I love you. And I had a wonderful time with you. But I can't pretend I don't care for Billy, because I do."

"I guess I thought that once we were together again for a few days, you might change your mind," Josh admitted.

"Even if Billy weren't in the picture," Carrie said, "I'd still want to be free to see other guys. I'm just not ready to settle down!"

"Yeah, well, it's not like you haven't told me that before," Josh said ruefully. "But I'm not going to be a chump about this, Car. It hurts too much. I'm going to start seeing other girls when I get back home."

Carrie couldn't believe the stab of pain that went through her heart. But fair was fair. "I understand," she said.

Josh gave her the saddest look. "I wish you didn't understand, babe. I wish the thought made you so insanely jealous that you'd be all mine again."

"I can't do that right now," Carrie whispered, tears in her eyes.

"I know," Josh said. He put his arms around her and held her tight. Carrie hugged him back with all her might. Why did life and love have to be so damned complicated, anyway?

Josh stood up and quickly wiped the traces of tears from his eyes. He pulled Carrie off the bed. "Drive me to the ferry?" he asked her.

Carrie nodded, staring hard at the face she knew and loved so well. "Just promise me this, Josh," she said tremulously. "Promise me that you won't ever stop being my friend. I couldn't stand that."

Josh put his arms around her and spoke in a low voice near her ear. "That will never happen, Carrie Alden. Never."

Carrie gulped back her tears. Even when you followed your heart, it was so difficult sometimes to know if you were doing the right thing. One decision could change your whole life, and how would you ever know what might have been if you'd chosen another road? Still, Carrie knew that all she could do was her best, and her best was what she was trying to do.

"Ready to go?" Josh asked, reaching for his suitcase.

"Ready," Carrie said firmly.

And whatever was to happen, Carrie felt like she really was.

ABOUT THE AUTHOR

As well as being a much-published, best-selling author of young-adult fiction, Cherie Bennett is an award-winning playwright, an actress, and a singer. She recently completed writing her first feature film for New Line Cinema. Cherie is married to attorney and theatrical producer Jeff Gottesfeld. After living for many years in New York City, they now reside in Nashville, Tennessee.

**Read how Carrie, Emma, and Sam
began their Sunset Island escapades.
Love. Laughter. Romance. Dreams come true,
and friendships last a lifetime.**

by Cherie Bennett

When Emma, Sam, and Carrie spend the summer working as au pairs on a resort island, they quickly become
allies in adventure!

__SUNSET ISLAND   0-425-12969-1/$3.50
__SUNSET KISS   0-425-12899-7/$3.50
__SUNSET DREAMS   0-425-13070-3/$3.50
__SUNSET FAREWELL   0-425-12772-9/$3.50
__SUNSET REUNION   0-425-13318-4/$3.50

For Visa, MasterCard and American Express orders ($10 minimum) call: 1-800-631-8571

FOR MAIL ORDERS: CHECK BOOK(S). FILL
OUT COUPON. SEND TO:

BERKLEY PUBLISHING GROUP
390 Murray Hill Pkwy., Dept. B
East Rutherford, NJ 07073

NAME_____

ADDRESS_____

CITY_____

STATE_____ZIP_____

PLEASE ALLOW 6 WEEKS FOR DELIVERY.
PRICES ARE SUBJECT TO CHANGE WITHOUT NOTICE.

POSTAGE AND HANDLING:
$1.50 for one book, 50¢ for each ad-
ditional. Do not exceed $4.50.

BOOK TOTAL $ _____

POSTAGE & HANDLING $ _____

APPLICABLE SALES TAX $ _____
(CA, NJ, NY, PA)

TOTAL AMOUNT DUE $ _____

PAYABLE IN US FUNDS.
(No cash orders accepted.)

366

*Sam, Carrie, and Emma return to Sunset
Island and their summer jobs as au pairs...*
Let the adventure begin!

By Cherie Bennett

___*SUNSET HEAT #7*   *0-425-13383-4/$3.50*

Sam is hired by a talent scout to dance in a show in Japan. Unfortunately, Emma
and Carrie don't share her enthusiasm. No one really knows if this is on the up
and up, especially after her fiasco with the shifty photographer last summer. But
Sam is determined to go despite her friends. . .

___*SUNSET PROMISES #8*   *0-425-13384-2/$3.50*

Carrie receives a lot of attention when she shows her photos at the Sunset Gallery.
She is approached by a publisher who wants her to do a book of pictures of the
island. But when Carrie photos the entire island, she discovers a part of Sunset
Island that tourists never see...

___*SUNSET SCANDAL #9 (August 1992)*   *0-425-13385-0/$3.50*

Emma has started to see Kurt again, and everything's going great...until Kurt is
arrested as the suspect in a rash of robberies! He has no alibi, and things look
pretty bad. Then, Emma befriends a new girl on the island who might be able to
help prove Kurt's innocence.

___*SUNSET WHISPERS #10 (September 1992)*   *0-425-13386-9/$3.50*

Sam is shocked to find out she is adopted. She's never needed her friends more
than when her birth mother comes to Sunset Island to meet her. And to add to
the chaos, Sam and Emma, along with the rest of the girls on the island, are
auditioning to be back up in the rock band *Flirting with Danger*.

For Visa, MasterCard and American Express orders ($10 minimum) call: 1-800-631-8571

FOR MAIL ORDERS: CHECK BOOK(S). FILL OUT COUPON. SEND TO:	POSTAGE AND HANDLING: $1.50 for one book, 50¢ for each additional. Do not exceed $4.50.
BERKLEY PUBLISHING GROUP 390 Murray Hill Pkwy., Dept. B East Rutherford, NJ 07073	BOOK TOTAL $ _____
NAME_____	POSTAGE & HANDLING $ _____
ADDRESS _____	APPLICABLE SALES TAX $ _____ (CA, NJ, NY, PA)
CITY_____	TOTAL AMOUNT DUE $ _____
STATE_____ZIP_____	PAYABLE IN US FUNDS.
PLEASE ALLOW 6 WEEKS FOR DELIVERY. PRICES ARE SUBJECT TO CHANGE WITHOUT NOTICE.	(No cash orders accepted.)